A Word from Stephanie
about Families

It all started when I met a new girl at school who was just like me. We had the same haircut and the same super-cool backpack, and we both liked to write. I just knew that Tamar and I would be good friends. Then it turned out we weren't just friends—we were cousins!

It was great to meet a new member of my family. There was only one problem: our fathers weren't talking! It turned out they had a big fight about twenty years ago and hadn't spoken since.

Tamar and I decided it was time for our fathers to make up. We planned a big Tanner family get-together. We told a reporter we would write an article about the reunion for a local magazine. Then the big day came—and the reunion was a total disaster!

Now my father is mad at me. Tamar won't even talk to me. And the magazine won't publish our story. I don't know what to do. I need some good advice—and fast!

Luckily there are plenty of people to ask for advice in my house. There are nine people and a dog living there. There's me, my big sister, D.J., my little sister, Michelle, and my dad, Danny. And that's just the beginning.

When my mom died, Dad needed help. So he asked his old college buddy, Joey Gladstone, and my uncle

Jesse to come live with us, to help take care of me and my sisters.

Back then, Uncle Jesse didn't know much about taking care of three girls. He was more into rock 'n' roll. Joey didn't know anything about kids, either—but it sure was fun watching him learn!

Having Uncle Jesse and Joey around was like having three dads instead of one! But then something even better happened—Uncle Jesse fell in love. He married Rebecca Donaldson, Dad's co-host on his TV show, *Wake Up, San Francisco*. Aunt Becky's so nice—she's more like a big sister than an aunt.

Next, Uncle Jesse and Aunt Becky had twin baby boys. Their names are Nicky and Alex, and they are adorable!

I love being part of a big family. Still, things can get pretty crazy when you live in such a full house!

FULL HOUSE™:
Stephanie novels

Available from MINSTREL Books

FULL HOUSE™
Stephanie

What Can You Grow
on a Family Tree?

Devra Newberger Speregen

A Parachute Book

A MINSTREL®
BOOK

Published by POCKET BOOKS
New York   London   Toronto   Sydney   Tokyo   Singapore

A MINSTREL PAPERBACK *Original*

A Minstrel Book published by
POCKET BOOKS, a division of Simon & Schuster Inc.
1230 Avenue of Americas, New York, NY 10020

A PARACHUTE BOOK

 Copyright © and ™ 1999 by Warner Bros.

FULL HOUSE, characters, names and all related indicia
are trademarks of Warner Bros. © 1999.

All rights reserved, including the right to reproduce
this book or portions thereof in any form whatsoever.
For information address Pocket Books, 1230 Avenue
of the Americas, New York, NY 10020

ISBN: 0–671–02162–1

First Minstrel Books printing August 1999

10 9 8 7 6 5 4 3 2 1

A MINSTREL BOOK and colophon are registered trademarks of
Simon & Schuster Inc.

Cover photo by Schultz Photography

Printed in the U.S.A.

QBP/✖

What Can You Grow on a Family Tree?

CHAPTER
1

"Stephanie, you would have *totally* cracked up!"

Stephanie Tanner laughed. "I can't believe I missed it, Allie!" she said to her best friend. "I would have loved to see you ride a donkey!"

Allie Taylor blew her dark brown bangs back from her face and reached into her locker for a book. "It was tons of fun," she said. "Maybe you can come with me to my next Taylor family reunion. My cousin Sarah is the greatest!"

Stephanie smiled, though she was only half-listening. Allie had returned from her New Mexico vacation three weeks before, and Stephanie had already heard all her vacation stories—some of them twice.

"By the way, Steph," Allie said, "that's a great haircut."

Stephanie pushed a lock of her thick blond hair behind one ear and grinned. She really liked her new hairstyle, too. It was the first time she had actually *loved* the way her hair looked. Just yesterday she had had it cut just above her shoulders with a side part. She liked wearing the longer side pulled across her forehead and tucked behind her ear. It made her feel older and more sophisticated.

"Thanks," she told Allie. Then she leaned back against her locker and peered down the hallway. "Hey! There's Darcy. *Darce!*" she called to their other best friend.

"Hey, guys!" Darcy skipped up to them and stopped. She had just gotten a haircut, too, and Stephanie thought it was awesome. Darcy's light brown curls were cropped close to her head, and with her smooth, dark complexion and bright hazel eyes, she looked a lot like the actress Jada Pinkett-Smith.

"Ready for social studies?" Darcy asked.

Stephanie and Allie both nodded. In a stroke of good luck, all three friends had managed to get the same second-period class this semester.

"I was just telling Stephanie about the coolest little jewelry shop in Santa Fe," Allie said as she tugged a large textbook out of her locker.

"Wait, don't tell me—let me guess," Darcy said with a grin. "Was this the jewelry shop where you and your cousin bought a pair of earrings to share?"

Stephanie felt a major urge to laugh. Allie had told them about the jewelry store three times already! Instead, she buried her head in her own locker and pretended to look for something important.

"I guess I already told you about it," Allie said with a shrug. "Still, the store was so-o-o amazing. They had this one necklace made of silver and—"

"Hang on a second," Darcy suddenly whispered. "You guys have *got* to check this out."

"What?" Stephanie asked. Even Allie stopped talking.

Darcy pointed down the hallway. "Look at that girl with the Sport-Glo backpack!"

"What? Where?" Stephanie's eyes darted from

person to person. Finally she noticed a girl with shoulder-length blond hair and a bright red Sport-Glo backpack—the exact same backpack as hers.

"Wow!" Allie exclaimed in shock. "Stephanie, that girl could be *you* from the back. Same height, same hair, same Sport-Glo and everything!"

"I thought those backpacks were, like, incredibly hard to find," Darcy commented.

Stephanie nodded as she adjusted her own Sport-Glo. "They are," she said. "I managed to get mine only because my father interviewed the designer on his TV show. I thought I was the only one in school with a Sport-Glo."

"Not anymore," Allie pointed out.

"It's weird how much she looks like you from the back," Darcy said.

Stephanie shrugged. "I don't exactly know what I look like from the back."

"Like that," Allie said, pointing at the girl with the Sport-Glo. "That girl could be your *from-the-back* twin!"

"Maybe she *is* your twin," Darcy joked. "Maybe you guys were separated at birth, like in the movie *The Parent Trap!*"

4

"Yeah!" Allie cried. "Maybe she grew up far, far away while you were growing up here in San Francisco. And now you're destined to meet . . ."

Stephanie rolled her eyes. "Give me a break, guys," she said with a laugh.

"Look! She's standing outside Leviton's room," Allie said. "Maybe she's in our class!"

"I hope so," Stephanie said, fishing her notebook out of her locker. "I'd really like to know how she managed to get a Sport-Glo."

Allie and Darcy followed Stephanie down the hall toward class. They reached the classroom just as the blond girl was about to head inside.

"Uh, excuse me!" Stephanie said loudly.

The girl turned to face them. "Who, me?" she asked.

Stephanie studied her face. The blond girl looked nothing like her. For one thing, this girl had about a zillion freckles. Stephanie didn't have any, unless you counted the small beauty mark on her temple.

Stephanie shot a look at Darcy. "*See?*" she said knowingly. "We're obviously *not* twins!"

The blond girl seemed confused. "Twins?" she asked.

Stephanie made a face. "My friends thought we were twins from the back," she said with a laugh. "You know, same hairstyle, same backpack."

The girl's eyes widened. "You have a Sport-Glo?" she asked.

Stephanie turned around to show off her backpack.

"How'd you get a Sport-Glo?" the girl asked her.

"My dad got it for me," Stephanie said.

The girl smiled. "My dad got mine for me, too!" she said.

"Okay, so you both have cool dads. But how come you guys have the same exact hairstyle?" Darcy teased.

"I get my hair cut downtown, at Off the Top," the girl said as she pulled the longer side behind her opposite ear.

"Hey! Me, too," Stephanie said with a laugh. "By Marissa," she added.

"Get out of here! Marissa cuts *my* hair!" the girl cried.

Darcy and Allie stared at them.

"Weird," Allie muttered. "What's your name, anyway?" she asked.

"And if you say Stephanie, I'm calling the five o'clock news!" Darcy put in.

The girl laughed. "No, it's Tamar. I guess *you're* Stephanie," she said to Stephanie.

Stephanie nodded. "Yup. These are my friends Darcy and Allie. Are you new or something?"

Tamar nodded. "Yeah. I used to go to Kennedy Middle School, but we moved and I switched school districts. This school is a little bigger than mine—I can barely find my classrooms! Are you guys in this social studies class?" she asked.

"Yes," Stephanie said. "Mr. Leviton's the best. You can sit with us if you want."

"Thanks," Tamar said. "What are you guys studying?"

"Mostly, we're learning American history," Stephanie told her, "but on Fridays and Mondays we have current events."

"Sounds cool," Tamar said, walking into the classroom.

Stephanie noticed a newspaper sticking out from Tamar's backpack. It looked like a school newspaper, but it wasn't the *Scribe.* It was called *Lines.*

"Lines?" Stephanie asked. "What's that?"

Tamar smiled. "Oh, that's just my old school's newspaper. I was the editor there."

Stephanie's eyes widened. "I can't believe this!" she exclaimed. "*I'm* the editor of the school paper *here!*"

Tamar grinned. "Really? You like to write?" she asked.

Stephanie laughed. "Do I like to write?" she repeated. She turned to Allie and Darcy, who were still obviously dumbstruck by the similarities between Tamar and their best friend. "Will you guys tell Tamar how much I *love* writing?"

"She loves writing," Darcy confirmed.

"In a big way," Allie added.

Tamar shook her head. "This is wild," she said. "We have so much in common. Hey, maybe we can have lunch together, too! I have it fifth period."

"Excellent! So do we," Stephanie said.

"You can sit at our table if you want," Darcy added. "And I bet you and Stephanie will have the exact same food for lunch."

Tamar nodded. "That would be great—I hate sitting alone. Thanks."

The girls all took their seats as Mr. Leviton called

roll. "Today, for Current Events Friday," he said when he was done, "I have a special surprise."

Stephanie exchanged excited looks with her friends. Mr. Leviton had a reputation at John Muir Middle School for giving awesome current events projects. Stephanie loved his assignments almost as much as she loved doing her stories for creative-writing class.

Mr. Leviton began handing out the *Teen Weekender.* Every other Friday he gave the class copies of the little magazine, which was filled with hip stories, fun places to go, great things to do, and current events—all just for teens in northern California.

"This is the coolest magazine," Stephanie whispered to Tamar as they were handed copies.

"Oh, I know," Tamar replied. "They have this at my old school, too."

"And today, class, we have a special guest," Mr. Leviton announced as Stephanie and her classmates began flipping through their copies. "I would like you to meet Sheryl Stetson. She's the editor in chief of *Teen Weekender.*"

Stephanie glanced up as a young woman with curly red hair rose from a chair at the front of the room.

"You'll be happy to know," Mr. Leviton went on, "that *Teen Weekender* has picked our school, from all the schools in northern California, to do an entire student-written issue!"

Stephanie's eyes widened with excitement.

"That's right," Sheryl Stetson said with a smile. "For this special issue, I'm looking for stories about teenagers and their families. Stories about interesting places teenagers have visited, that sort of thing."

I can do that, Stephanie thought happily. *I've got plenty of stories about my family.*

"I'll choose the best story idea from each class in the school," Miss Stetson went on. "So every class will have an article in the magazine. And the best idea of all will be chosen as the cover story. The student who writes it will get his or her picture on the front cover. Now this has to be done quickly. Your stories are due a week from Monday and the John Muir issue will be out on that next Friday."

Stephanie listened carefully. It all sounded too good to be true. She tried to imagine what it would be like to appear on the cover of *Teen Weekender.* It would be *unbelievable.*

"Stephanie, did you hear that?" Allie whispered. "You must have a *zillion* ideas for a good article. You'll get the cover story for sure!"

"Yeah, if anyone has story ideas, it's you. You're the best journalist in the whole school," Darcy added.

Stephanie's eyes twinkled. She was already lost in thought—her mind working overtime.

Allie and Darcy are right, she thought. *How hard can it be to come up with a great story idea?*

Stephanie glanced over at Darcy and gave her the thumbs-up. *Look out,* Teen Weekender, she thought. *You have a new cover girl—Stephanie Tanner!*

CHAPTER
2

◆ ◀ ✦ ◆

"Stephanie! Phone for you!" Joey Gladstone called up the stairs that evening. Joey was Stephanie's father's best friend.

"Thanks, Joey," Stephanie called down. She walked over to the phone in her room.

Joey hollered back in his best British accent, "At your service, madam."

Stephanie rolled her eyes and laughed. Joey was such a goofball. "Hello?" she said into the phone.

"Stephanie? This is Tamar."

"Tamar, hi!"

"Was that your dad?" Tamar asked.

"No, that was his friend, Joey," Stephanie replied. "My father is in Chicago on business this week."

"Wow, are you staying all by yourself?" Tamar asked.

"Uh, I think it would be hard to stay by myself in this house," Stephanie told her.

It was true. There was always somebody around in the Tanner house—there were nine people and a dog living there!

After Stephanie's mother died, Joey had moved in with the Tanners to help out with Stephanie and her two sisters, D.J. and Michelle. He lived in an apartment in the basement, and he was practically a part of the family now. Plus, Stephanie's uncle, Jesse, also lived with them. He shared the attic apartment with his wife, Becky, and their twin sons, Nicky and Alex.

"I know how you feel," Tamar said. "Between me and my brothers, my house is always crowded. Do you have two brothers, too, Stephanie?"

"Aha!" Stephanie cried. "Finally something we *don't* have in common. I don't have any brothers. I have two *sisters*, though. I'm the middle sister."

"Me, too. I mean, I'm in the middle, too," Tamar said. "Don't you hate it? It's like you're never old enough, or you're *too* old—know what I mean?"

"Absolutely," Stephanie replied. "And the oldest and youngest always get away with everything!"

Tamar nodded. "Doesn't it drive you nuts?"

"Bonkers!" Stephanie answered.

She couldn't believe how great Tamar was. She was sure they were going to become good friends. At lunch they had discovered that they had English class together, too. So Stephanie would see Tamar for three periods every day!

"I was thinking, Stephanie," Tamar said. "Since you and I are both editors and we both love to write, and since we have so much in common, maybe we should work together on a story for the *Teen Weekender.*"

Stephanie considered that. She usually wrote alone, but she wanted to get that cover story for the magazine . . .

"Well, two newspaper editors must surely be better than one," she said slowly.

"Absolutely," Tamar agreed. "If we put our

brains together, we'll definitely come up with a story idea good enough for the cover."

Stephanie hesitated. What if Tamar wanted to write a story on something Stephanie didn't care about?

"What do you say?" Tamar asked.

She sounded so cheerful and excited—and Stephanie really wanted to spend more time with her new friend.

"We'll brainstorm all night tonight if we have to!" Tamar added.

Why not? If we don't agree on a subject, I can always come up with something else on my own, Stephanie decided.

"I have a better idea," she told Tamar. "Let's meet at the mall tomorrow, and then we can brainstorm all *weekend* if we have to!"

That night Stephanie sat on the carpet in the bedroom she shared with her younger sister, Michelle. Piles and piles of family photo albums were stacked around her. She had hoped to begin working on some story ideas for the *Teen Weekender,* but first she needed to do an English project, a photo essay, which was due on Monday.

Stephanie marveled at how organized all the family photos were. Just another example of her father's need to keep everything neat. Five hundred pictures of Stephanie and her sisters—birthdays, Christmases, family vacations—were all dated, numbered, catalogued, and labeled in neat, organized photo albums.

"What are you doing, Steph?" Michelle asked as she came into the room. Michelle was ten years old and could often be more than a little nosy. This time Stephanie didn't mind. In fact, she was glad Michelle had come along. She could use a little help picking photographs.

"It's my English project," Stephanie explained. "I have to do a photo essay about somebody who was influential in my life."

"What's a photo essay?" Michelle asked.

"It's when you use photos instead of words to tell a story," Stephanie told her. "That's why I have all these photo albums. I'm trying to find some good pictures of Dad. I chose Dad because he's been the most influential person in my life."

Michelle picked up a large photo album and pointed to a picture of her father with Uncle Jesse and Joey.

"How about this one?" she asked.

Stephanie looked closely at the photo. It was a nice one—it had been taken on a family trip to San Diego right after Uncle Jesse had moved in with them. Somehow it wasn't right for her photo essay, though.

"No, that one won't work," she said. "I need pictures that tell a story. They have to show *why* dad is an influence on me." She went back to looking through the photo album in her lap.

"Oh," Michelle said. "Then what about this one?"

Stephanie glanced up again. Michelle was pointing to a photo of the whole family—her and her two sisters, their father, Uncle Jesse, Aunt Becky and their twins, and Joey. It was taken a few Christmases earlier.

Stephanie sighed. "Michelle, that picture doesn't tell a story. Don't you understand?"

"Yes," Michelle replied defensively. "It *does* tell a story. Don't you remember? Right after this picture was taken, Cousin Nicky fell on the coffee table and knocked his tooth out."

Stephanie stared at her sister in exasperation. "Yeah, so? What does that have to do with Dad being an influence in my life?"

"Well," Michelle went on, "*Dad* was the one who drove Nicky to the hospital, remember?"

"And?" Stephanie asked.

Michelle frowned. "Okay. I guess I *don't* understand."

Stephanie laughed. She knew her little sister was only trying to help.

"That picture *does* tell a good story," she offered gently, "but it's not exactly the kind of story I was thinking of for this—"

Suddenly Stephanie saw what she was searching for. She leaned over the album in her lap and lifted up the protective plastic page to get a better look at one of the photos.

"Michelle, check this out!"

Michelle moved closer and leaned over the album.

Stephanie carefully separated the photo from its sticky page. "It's a picture of Dad when he was in high school, working on the school newspaper!"

"That's Dad?" Michelle said in disbelief. "No way!"

"It is, really," Stephanie said. "He was so young! I don't know who this other guy is, though."

"I can't believe that's Dad! He looks . . . so *funny!*" Michelle exclaimed. She turned the page in the photo album. "Look, here are some more pictures of him with that guy."

Stephanie studied the album. There were nearly fifteen pictures of her father and the same guy.

"Do you know what this means, Michelle?" Stephanie asked excitedly.

Michelle shrugged. "No, what?" she asked.

"It means I have my photo essay!" Stephanie exclaimed. "These pictures are perfect! If I put them in order, I can show how hard Dad worked at his school paper and how he won writing awards and everything. Then I can show some pictures of me at my school paper. It will be totally obvious that I was influenced by Dad. It will be great!"

Michelle grinned. "I get it now," she said. "So everyone will see that you work on your school paper because Dad worked on his."

"Sort of," Stephanie said.

"Glad I could help," Michelle said, standing.

Stephanie began taking all the pictures of her father out of the album.

"Dad will flip out if you mess up his photo

albums," Michelle reminded her as she got ready for bed. "Shouldn't you wait until he comes home from his trip before you start pulling out those pictures?"

"I'm being careful," Stephanie told her. "And, anyway, it *can't* wait until he's home. I need to hand this project in on Monday. Dad won't be home until Monday!"

"So are you going to cut out that other guy from all the pictures?" Michelle asked as she pulled her pajama top over her head.

Stephanie thought about that. Dad's friend was in every single picture. She didn't even know who he was, though he looked sort of familiar.

"It would look pretty stupid if I cut him out from all of these," Stephanie replied. "I'll just leave him in, I guess."

As Michelle went to the bathroom to clean up, Stephanie picked up an armful of the photo albums to carry back to the hall closet. Her older sister D.J. came flying into the bedroom before she had taken two steps.

"Deej, what are you doing here so late?" Stephanie asked.

D.J. pulled her backpack off her shoulders, then dug into the front pocket of it. Finally she pulled out a set of keys and tossed them to Stephanie. Stephanie wasn't ready for the toss, so the keys fell to the floor with a thud.

"Steph! You *have* to help me out!" D.J. said breathlessly. "I'm in such a jam!"

"What's the matter?" Stephanie asked. She picked up the keys and turned them over in her hand. They didn't look like D.J.'s keys. "Whose are these?" she asked.

D.J. took a second to catch her breath. "Gladys Rowan's," she replied.

"Rowan?" Stephanie asked. "You mean our neighbor?"

D.J. nodded. "Steph, you really have to help me out! I missed two of my sociology classes because I had the flu and I'm so far behind!"

Stephanie was confused. "But what do you want *me* to do?" she asked.

"I need you to water Mrs. Rowan's plants," D.J. explained. "She's away for two weeks, and she asked me to do it for her, and I said I would, but then I got sick and now there's this study group on campus tonight that I can't miss! Will you do it?"

"Water her plants?" Stephanie repeated.

"Yes. And her rose garden outside, too." D.J.'s bright blue eyes were pleading. "Please, oh, please, oh, please?"

Stephanie groaned. "I guess," she said. "If it's just this one time—"

"Well, not exactly," D.J. murmured.

Stephanie stared at her. "What do you mean, not exactly?" she demanded.

D.J. ran her fingers through her short blond hair. "I need you to help me out for the weekend," she blurted out.

Stephanie's eyes widened. "The *whole* weekend?" she asked in disbelief.

D.J. nodded. "Come on, Steph! It won't be that bad! It's just once a day! I want to stay on campus this weekend. It will be such a pain if I have to keep coming back just to water her plants."

Stephanie folded her arms across her chest. "Well, you should have thought about that before you agreed to take the job."

"I'll pay you," D.J. offered. "Double. Just say you'll do this one, itsy-bitsy favor for me. Please? Pretty please?"

"Yeah, okay—" Stephanie began.

"Excellent!" D.J. cried. She pulled on her back-pack and headed for the door.

"Hey, wait!" Stephanie called after her.

D.J. stopped at the door. "What is it, Stephanie? I'm already so late!"

Stephanie showed her sister the picture of their father in high school. "Do you know who this guy is?" she asked.

"Yeah, that's Dad," D.J. replied. She let out a small laugh. "He looks so dorky, don't you think?"

Stephanie rolled her eyes. "I *know* that's Dad! I mean, do you know who the other guy is?"

D.J. sighed and took a closer look at the photo. She shrugged. "Nope. No idea. Anything else?"

Stephanie took back the picture and frowned. "No," she said, leaning against the doorway. She watched D.J. turn and race down the steps.

"Oh, I almost forgot!" D.J. shouted from the front door.

Stephanie ran into the hall and leaned over the railing. "Forgot what?" she asked.

"Mrs. Rowan has a cat!" D.J. yelled. "Give it fresh water and food every day. And be careful not to let it out when you go in!"

Stephanie made a face. She was not a huge fan of cats. She was more of a dog person.

"Yeah, all right!" she replied. "But you owe me," she added. "Big time!"

Stephanie headed back to her room to get ready for bed. She wanted to get to sleep early because she was supposed to meet Tamar at the mall first thing in the morning.

"What's with all the yelling?" Stephanie heard someone ask as she was about to close the door to her room. "What's going on?"

Stephanie poked her head back in the hall and saw Uncle Jesse. He was standing in the hallway next to the door leading up to his apartment.

"Nothing," she answered. "D.J. was just asking for a favor. As usual."

Jesse made a face. "Well, the twins just fell asleep, so can you be a little quieter? Becky and I are taking them to buy shoes tomorrow, and I *don't* want a pair of cranky boys tearing up the shoe store."

"No problem," Stephanie replied. "D.J. left anyway."

"Okay." Jesse turned to head back upstairs.

"Oh, wait, Uncle Jesse!" Stephanie called.

Jesse grimaced and held a finger to his lips.

"Oops. Sorry," Stephanie whispered. "I wanted to ask you something." She handed him the picture of her father and Jesse let out a chuckle.

"Look at Danny!" he scoffed. "What was with that hairstyle?"

Stephanie took another look at the photograph and let out a giggle herself. *Come to think of it,* she thought, *Dad's hair* did *look sort of goofy!*

"Uncle Jesse, do you know who the guy is with—"

Before she could finish, Jesse thrust the photo back at her. "No," he said in a strange voice. "I have to get back upstairs."

Stephanie watched, dumbfounded, as her uncle leapt back up to his apartment. She wanted to call after him, but she didn't want to wake her little cousins.

Boy, that was weird, she thought. She was sure she saw a hint of recognition on her uncle's face when he looked at the photo. Why had he acted so strangely?

Stephanie took another look at the picture.

The mystery man had to be *somebody* important.

After all, he was in more than a dozen pictures with her dad.

She stared at the photo a while longer. *Strange,* she thought, *he does look a little familiar.*

She wondered who he was.

And what all the secrecy was about.

CHAPTER
3

◆ ◀ ✦ ◆

Saturday morning Stephanie fumbled with Mrs. Rowan's keys and tried for the tenth time to open the front door to her house.

"Come on!" she shouted at the keys. "Open already."

She'd been standing in front of the house for fifteen minutes, trying to open the front door. She wondered if maybe D.J. had given her the wrong keys.

Finally Stephanie heard a *click* inside the lock. The key had worked.

"It's about time!" she exclaimed. She turned it all the way and pushed the door open.

Just then Mrs. Rowan's enormous cat appeared out of nowhere and tried to sneak through the doorway.

"Oh, no, you don't!" Stephanie commanded it. "You're not going anywhere. D.J. warned me about you."

Stephanie grimaced and wrapped her arms around the orange and white cat. She lifted the cat, which was a lot heavier than she expected, and managed to haul it back inside the house. Quickly she closed the door.

Once inside, Stephanie glanced around the house. She'd never been inside before. She decided it was sort of nice—except for the cat smell.

Then Stephanie noticed all the plants. There must have been dozens of them! She couldn't believe how many plants the Rowans had!

Is D.J. nuts? she wondered. *Watering all these plants is going to take forever!*

She was supposed to meet Tamar at the bus to go to the mall in twenty minutes.

Grumbling, Stephanie filled the ceramic pitcher with water. Then, as quickly as she could, she started watering. She knew she should probably be giving each plant more water than she was, but there simply wasn't enough time.

"I'll just give them extra tomorrow," she figured.

By the time she was finished, she had watered nearly forty plants. "It's like a forest in here," she said in disbelief. "How can anybody have so many plants?"

Next, it was time to feed the cat. Not that Mrs. Rowan's fat cat looked as though it *needed* food! "You must weigh a ton and a half," Stephanie said to the cat as she searched for a can of cat food. "You should go on a diet."

Stephanie fed the cat, filled its water bowl, then glanced at her watch. If she left right that minute, she would just make it to the bus stop on time.

That was when she remembered the roses!

The roses will just have to wait 'till tomorrow, she thought, hoping the lack of water wouldn't kill them or anything. *It's not my fault,* she reasoned with herself. *D.J. should have told me how many plants Mrs. Rowan had.*

After making sure Mrs. Rowan's cat was inside, Stephanie grabbed her bag and locked the front door. Then she ran the whole three blocks to the bus stop.

Tamar was already there and Stephanie was suddenly glad she was not late. She always *hated* when people were late for things. It wouldn't have been cool to leave a brand-new friend waiting.

"Hey!" Stephanie said breathlessly. "I ran all the way here."

"I just got here a few minutes ago," Tamar told her.

"I *would* have been here earlier," Stephanie added, "but my sister asked me to do her this big favor and it took *forever*. I'm usually early."

At that moment the bus to the mall pulled up in front of them. Stephanie followed Tamar up the steps and down the aisle to an empty seat in the back.

"So, anyway," Stephanie continued, "I told D.J. I would water the neighbors' plants for her, but when I got to the house, there were like a *million* plants. D.J. never told me the place was a jungle."

Tamar laughed. "Sounds like D.J. totally took advantage of you," she said.

Stephanie thought about that. Tamar was right. In fact, D.J. had been taking advantage of her in a lot of ways lately.

"Just because she's in college, she thinks her life

is so much more important than mine," Stephanie complained. "It's not fair. I have a life, too!"

"I know what you mean," Tamar replied. "My older brother, Brian, takes advantage of me all the time. He's always making me do his chores and run errands and stuff because he claims he's too busy with schoolwork. Like *I* don't have a ton of homework to do!"

"Tell me about it," Stephanie folded her arms across her chest and sat back in her seat.

It felt nice to have someone understanding to complain to for a change. She usually confided in Allie and Darcy, but they didn't have older brothers or sisters, so they couldn't really relate. Tamar could totally understand how annoying an older sibling can be.

"Hey, all this talk about schoolwork reminds me," Tamar said suddenly. "Did you start that photo essay for English yet?"

Stephanie brightened. She was only too happy to change the subject anyway.

"Yes, I started it last night," she said excitedly. "I found some awesome pictures of my dad in an old photo album. Pictures from when he worked on the school newspaper."

Tamar smiled. "Wow, that's great! You're so lucky. I looked through a few of our family albums, but I couldn't find anything good. My dad worked on his school paper, too, but I guess he didn't take any pictures!"

"The pictures of my dad are so funny," Stephanie told her. "His clothes and hair look really nerdy! Still, I think he was cute."

"I'd love to see it," Tamar said.

"Hang on a sec," Stephanie replied. "I have one of the pictures with me." She pulled her bag off her shoulder and began digging through the contents, searching for the photo.

"It's kind of strange," she said as she looked. "In every picture, my dad is with the same guy, but no one in my family knows who the guy is. He looks familiar, so I'm going to carry it around with me all weekend until I can figure out who he reminds me of. Now where is that photo?"

"Check the front pocket," Tamar suggested. "I always forget to look there."

Stephanie unzipped the big pocket on the front of her Sport-Glo. "You're right—here it is!" she cried. She pulled out the photo and handed it to Tamar.

Tamar glanced at the picture and laughed. "Your dad looks like one of those guys from *The Brady Bunch!*" she exclaimed. Then a strange expression crept over her face. Tamar's eyes suddenly grew very big, and her mouth fell open.

"Tamar? What is it?" Stephanie asked. "Are you choking or something?" Tamar kept staring at the picture, shaking her head in disbelief.

"Tamar?" Stephanie asked again. "What's going on?"

Finally Tamar faced Stephanie. "Stephanie!" she said slowly, this guy with your father . . ."

"The mystery man? What? What about him?" Stephanie asked.

"He's *my* father!"

33

CHAPTER
4

♦ ◄ ⭑ ♦

"What?" Stephanie cried.

Had she heard correctly? Did Tamar just say that the man in the picture was *her father?* How could that be?

Tamar pointed to the photograph. "Stephanie, I know this is my dad! He looks like this in his wedding pictures."

Stephanie grabbed the picture from her friend. "Are you positive?" she asked, studying the mystery man more closely. A chill ran through her as she realized why he'd looked so familiar. It was because he looked like—*Tamar!*

"You look like him," she commented.

"Everyone says that," Tamar said.

Stephanie shook her head in shock. "This is unbelievable!" she exclaimed. "Our fathers knew each other."

Tamar grinned. "This is so wild! Maybe they were really close friends!"

Stephanie nodded. "Maybe they were best friends!" she said. "What's your dad's name?"

"Ben," Tamar told her. "What about your father?"

"Danny," Stephanie replied. "I wonder why my father never told me about your father," she added. "I mean, there are all these pictures of them together, but he's never mentioned a friend named Ben before."

Tamar shrugged. "I don't know. My dad's never mentioned a Danny, either."

Stephanie looked back at the photo and sighed. "Maybe they lost touch a long time ago," she suggested. "It's too bad—we could have met back when we were babies."

Tamar laughed. "That would have been cool."

The bus pulled up to the mall entrance, and Stephanie slipped the picture back into the front pocket of her bag. As she stepped off the bus and through the mall entrance, she was struck by a thought.

"Hey! I have an awesome idea!" she exclaimed.

Tamar followed her into the mall. "What is it?" she asked.

"My father is coming back from his business trip to New York on Monday," Stephanie explained. "Why don't you and your father come over for dinner? I won't tell my dad about it, so he'll be surprised."

Tamar grinned. "That's an excellent idea. I won't say anything to my father either. It will be like a big secret reunion!"

The girls walked through the mall and headed for the strip of clothing shops at the far end.

Just wait until Dad sees Ben! Stephanie thought as they walked. *He's going to be so happy I've found his long-lost buddy!*

To her surprise, Stephanie found Uncle Jesse in front of the Little Feet shoe store. Aunt Becky stood next to him, holding Nicky and Alex by their hands.

"Hey, there's my uncle," Stephanie said to Tamar. She called to Jesse. "Uncle Jesse! Over here!"

Jesse glanced up. Then he smiled and waved the girls over.

"How did shoe shopping go?" Stephanie asked.

"Not bad," Becky replied. "We managed to buy them each two pairs before things got crazy."

"Look at my *choos*, Cousin Stephanie!" Alex said, proudly kicking his foot in Stephanie's direction.

"Wow! They're very beautiful," Stephanie exclaimed.

Alex frowned. "No! Not *bootiful*," he said. "Cool! Daddy said my choos are cool!"

"That's right, sport!" Jesse said, ruffling Alex's hair. "So, who is your friend, Stephanie? You look familiar," he added, studying Tamar's face. "Have we met before?"

"No," Tamar told him. "I transferred to Stephanie's school last week."

"We have social studies and English together," Stephanie said. "And guess what else, Uncle Jesse. Dad and Tamar's father used to be friends!"

Jesse's eyes widened. "Huh?" he asked.

Stephanie reached into her bag and pulled out the photograph.

"This picture! The one I showed you last night. I know who the mystery man is now—it's Tamar's *father!* They were friends. Isn't that awesome?"

Jesse took the photo from Stephanie and reexamined it. Then he stared at Tamar again. "This is unbelievable," he said quietly.

"Isn't it?" Stephanie exclaimed. "It's freaky! I just met Tamar yesterday and we have so much in common, and then it turns out our fathers were best buds back in high school. I mean, what are the chances of that happening?"

Stephanie noticed Jesse and Becky exchange glances.

"So I was thinking," she went on, "that it would be fun to get them together again. Tamar and I are going to plan a surprise reunion dinner for them. Isn't that great?"

Jesse didn't answer. He just kept staring back and forth between the picture and Tamar.

"So what do you think?" Stephanie pressed. "Won't Dad be happy when he sees his long-lost friend in our kitchen? I can't wait to see his face."

"Uh, I don't think that's such a good idea, Steph," Jesse said slowly.

"What?" Stephanie asked in confusion. "Why not?"

Jesse thrust the photo back at Stephanie. "It's just not, okay? Trust me—you should drop the whole idea. Come on, guys," he said to Nicky and Alex. "Let's go visit the toy store before lunch."

Stephanie and Tamar exchanged surprised looks.

What in the world is going on? Stephanie wondered. *Uncle Jesse is acting weird again, just like last night when I showed him the picture.*

"We'll see you back at home," Jesse said as he ushered the boys in the opposite direction.

"Hey, wait," Stephanie called after him. "Uncle Jesse! Don't leave. What's going on?"

Jesse turned around. "Look, Stephanie. I can't go into it right now, okay? You should . . . maybe you should ask your father. Forget about the reunion dinner, though. It's really not a good idea."

Stephanie stared at her uncle in shock. *This is nuts!* she thought angrily. *Something is going on, and nobody is telling me anything!*

"Hold on a second!" she cried. "This is not fair! I don't know what the big secret is, but I want you to tell me why you're acting so weird. If this has anything to do with my dad, then I have a right to know."

Jesse and Becky looked at each other again.

"Aunt Becky?" Stephanie asked. "Tell me— please? Uncle Jesse?"

After a moment Jesse let out a deep sigh. "Okay, Stephanie," he said quietly. "Here's the deal. Tamar is not your friend."

Stephanie heard Tamar give a little gasp.

"What are you talking about?" Stephanie demanded.

"Tamar is *more* than just your friend," Jesse explained. "She's your *cousin*."

CHAPTER
5

◆　◀　◆　◆

"Cousins?" Stephanie and Tamar cried at the same time.

"I don't understand," Stephanie added.

Jesse ran his fingers through his hair. "Well, you're *second* cousins, actually," he corrected himself. "Your father and Tamar's father are first cousins."

Stephanie looked at Tamar. She could tell by the expression on her friend's face that all this was news to her, too.

"How come nobody ever told me I had second cousins?" Stephanie asked. "How come I never met Tamar until now?"

"I never knew about you, either," Tamar said. "Why?"

Both girls gazed up at Jesse, waiting for answers.

"Okay, I'll tell you as much as I know. Back in high school, your fathers *were* best buds," Jesse explained. "They were always together. Stephanie, your mother once told me Danny and Ben were more like brothers than cousins. I never knew Ben," Jesse added. "Your father and my sister got married almost four years after the 'Big Cousins Incident.'"

Stephanie frowned in confusion. "The *what?*" she asked.

"That's what Danny always called it," Jesse explained. "The Big Cousins Incident. Anyway, after the Big Cousins Incident, your fathers never spoke again."

Stephanie's mouth fell open. "Are you serious?" she asked.

Jesse nodded.

"But why?" Tamar asked. "What happened?"

Jesse shrugged. "I'm not one hundred percent sure," he said. "But, Steph, your mom always said it was because of something really dumb."

"That doesn't make any sense," Stephanie said. "How can something dumb make two cousins not speak ever again?"

"Well, you know how stubborn Tanners can be," Jesse remarked.

"No kidding," Stephanie and Tamar said in unison.

Stephanie spun around to Tamar. "Wait a minute!" she cried. "Is your last name Tanner?"

Tamar nodded. "Yes! I thought you knew my last name was Tanner. Is *your* last name Tanner?"

Stephanie nodded. "This is wild."

Tamar let out a laugh. "It's incredible."

"Boy, wait until Allie and Darcy hear this!"

"So, you see why making a surprise dinner for your dads might not be such a great idea?" Jesse asked. "Maybe you should talk to them first."

Stephanie sighed. "I guess," she said glumly. "But it's so unfair! How come Tamar and I have to suffer because of something that happened like, a hundred years ago?"

"Do you even have a tiny clue as to what the Big Cousins Incident was about?" Tamar asked Jesse.

Jesse shook his head. "Nope. Danny has always

refused to talk about it. All I know is high school graduation day was the last time Danny and Ben Tanner ever spoke to each other."

"Wow," Stephanie muttered. "It's all so unbelievable."

"Jesse," Becky said gently. "The boys are getting restless."

"Okay. I'm coming," Jesse told her. He put a hand on Stephanie's shoulder. "When you first showed me the picture last night, I thought I could get away with not telling you anything. But now that you've met Tamar, everything has changed. You want to know more about your cousin, and I understand that. But it's not my place to say anything. You're going to have to ask your father."

Stephanie nodded. Uncle Jesse was right. After all, *he* wasn't the one who'd kept the secret from her all these years.

"Thanks, Uncle Jesse," she told him.

"Yeah, thanks, Uncle Jesse," Tamar said. "Hey, are you *my* uncle, too?" she asked.

Jesse smiled. "No, but you can call me Uncle Jesse if you want," he said.

Tamar grinned. "Cool! Thanks."

"Toy store!" Nicky yelled.

"Oops! Better get going. I'll see you later, girls," Jesse said.

Stephanie watched her uncle and his family disappear into the Fun Stuff toy store. When he was gone, she turned to Tamar.

"Can you believe it? We're cousins!" she cried.

Tamar gave her a hug. "It's like a dream come true," she said. "I've always wished for a sister—but a cousin is just as cool!"

"I've never wished for another sister," Stephanie said with a laugh, "but I have wished for a family member my own age."

"Talk about a weird story," Tamar commented. "The fact that our dads are cousins—and we didn't even know it when we became friends!"

"Yeah, it is a weird story," Stephanie agreed. Then she realized what she had just said. Her eyes widened and a huge grin broke across her face.

"That's the key word!" she told Tamar.

Tamar seemed confused. "What is?" she asked.

"*Story!* Our being cousins makes a *great* story. You know—a story that could, oh, I don't know— make a great *magazine article!*"

Tamar's eyes twinkled. "Stephanie Tanner, what are you thinking?"

"Same thing *you're* thinking, Tamar Tanner!" Stephanie replied. "I think we've just found our story idea for the *Teen Weekender!* Picture this headline: LONG-LOST SECOND COUSINS FIND EACH OTHER COMPLETELY BY CHANCE!"

Tamar squealed with delight. "Or what about COUSINS REUNITED BY CLASS PROJECT!"

Stephanie laughed. "That's great!" Then she had another idea. "Wait. I just thought of something even *better* than that!"

She felt herself smiling from ear to ear. "I have a story idea that will get us on the cover of *Teen Weekender* for sure!"

CHAPTER
6

◆ ◀ ✦ ◆

Stephanie fell onto a nearby mall bench. Her mind was racing. Tamar sat next to her.

"Stephanie, we haven't known each other for very long," Tamar remarked, "but I can already tell when something huge is going on in your head! Exactly what are you cooking up in that wild Tanner imagination of yours?"

Stephanie smiled mysteriously. "I'm thinking," she said slowly, "of something Allie told me."

"What?" Tamar asked.

"Well, all Allie talks about lately is how much fun she had at her family reunion."

"So?" Tamar prompted.

"So I'm thinking about a Tanner family reunion!" Stephanie announced.

"A family reunion?"

"Yes. It's the perfect story idea!" Stephanie insisted. "Don't you think?"

"It *is* an awesome idea," Tamar agreed. "What about your Uncle Jesse? You told him you wouldn't try to get our dads together."

"I know, I know." Stephanie sighed. "But I think Uncle Jesse is *wrong.* If our dads were as close as he said they were, then they would probably be *happy* to see each other again after all these years."

Tamar nodded. "It's been so long, they've probably forgotten why they were mad in the first place."

"Right!" Stephanie exclaimed. "And they probably miss each other like crazy. Once they see each other, they'll probably hug and say how stupid they've been to stay mad."

"Then I think we should do it," Tamar declared.

"Me, too. I bet our fathers will even *thank* us for it!" Stephanie added.

Tamar held out her fist. "Then it's settled?" she asked. "The secret reunion dinner is on?"

Stephanie hit her fist on top of Tamar's. "Definitely," she said excitedly. "But forget the dinner part. I think we should have a Tanner family reunion during the day with all the trimmings. A big picnic with lots of food and fun and potato sack races—next Saturday."

"Cool! But do you think Miss Stetson will like the reunion idea enough to pick it for the cover?" Tamar asked.

Stephanie took a deep breath and pictured the joyous, teary, hugs-and-kisses reunion she and Tamar would plan for their fathers.

It was just the kind of tug-at-the-heartstrings stuff magazines were always *full* of.

Stephanie grinned confidently at her second cousin. "Oh, I think it'll be front-page material for sure!" she proclaimed.

"Guess what?" Stephanie said to Allie and Darcy on Monday at lunch.

Her best friends exchanged confused looks. "What?" Allie asked.

Stephanie grinned at Tamar. "You tell them," she suggested.

Tamar put down the sandwich she was eating.

"Well, on Saturday Stephanie and I found out something amazing."

"We're cousins!" Stephanie announced.

Darcy and Allie both looked so surprised that Stephanie burst out laughing. Tamar joined in.

"Cousins! I can't believe it," Darcy said, her dark eyes shining. She crumpled up her lunch bag and tossed it in a nearby garbage can. "That is so cool!"

"I knew you guys had to be related *somehow*," Allie added, tossing her paper bag in the trash after Darcy. "You're so alike."

Stephanie nudged Tamar. "Should we tell them *everything?*" she asked her cousin.

Tamar nodded enthusiastically. "Sure."

Allie's eyes narrowed. "Tell us *what?*" she asked.

Darcy leaned forward on the cafeteria table. "Yeah, tell us what? You two have been acting suspiciously all during lunch. What's going on?"

Stephanie's eyes twinkled. "We have a secret," she sang.

"A really awesome secret," Tamar added.

Darcy groaned. "Both of you are getting to be so annoying. Will you just tell us already?"

"Okay, okay!" Stephanie agreed. "But you can't tell anybody else yet—Tamar and I want to tell everyone. Only we have to wait for the official okay."

"We promise!" Allie insisted.

Stephanie took a deep breath. "Our story is going to be on the cover of *Teen Weekender!*"

Darcy and Allie both gasped.

"You're kidding!" Darcy said.

"How do you know?" Allie asked. "Everyone submitted their story ideas this morning."

"Well," Stephanie explained, "after class Tamar and I had a secret meeting with Miss Stetson and Mr. Leviton, and—"

"A secret meeting?" Allie asked. "Isn't that a little dramatic?"

"Okay, so it wasn't exactly a big secret," Stephanie admitted, "but it was still *private*. Anyway, you see, when Tamar and I found out we were second cousins, we also found out why we never knew about each other before. We didn't tell you that part."

Allie and Darcy exchanged looks.

"It turns out," Tamar continued, "our fathers had this big blowup back in high school and they never spoke to each other again."

Darcy's eyes widened. "Are you serious?"

Stephanie and Tamar both nodded.

"What was the fight about?" Allie asked.

"We don't know," Stephanie replied. "See, my dad doesn't know that I've met Tamar, because he's been in New York on business. Also, Tamar hasn't told her dad about me."

Darcy sat back in her seat. "Wow," she said. "They haven't spoken to each other in twenty years?"

Stephanie nodded. "Crazy, isn't it?"

"I had a fight with my cousin last Easter, but we made up in about an hour," Darcy commented.

"Well, Tamar and I both think that once our fathers see each other they'll forget about the silly fight and become close again, like they used to be."

"So we're going to have a surprise reunion," Tamar blurted out, "and capture the whole thing on film for the cover story."

Stephanie nodded eagerly. "Miss Stetson thought our story idea was great. She even sort of promised us the cover."

"Sort of?" Allie asked.

Stephanie wrinkled up her nose. "Well, she said

she still needed to look over all the story ideas, but that ours was really great."

"So it's not definite," Darcy said.

"It's almost definite," Stephanie told her.

Darcy and Allie didn't answer.

"Come on. Isn't it the best idea ever?" Stephanie demanded.

"I don't know, Steph," Darcy said cautiously. "How are you ever going to arrange a big family reunion anyway?"

Stephanie rolled her eyes. "How hard can it be?"

"And what about all those *other* things—you know, like *homework?* Chores? Mrs. Holtz's English test?" Allie pointed out.

"Piece of cake!" Stephanie exclaimed.

Tamar agreed. "We already picked a nice park for the reunion, and we're going to make lots of sandwiches," she added. "It's going to be a blast!"

"And what happens if your fathers aren't happy to see each other?" Allie asked. "Then the only 'blast' is going to be from their car tailpipes as they both drive away."

"That's not going to happen," Stephanie assured her. "They're going to be happy to see each other. They used to be best friends!"

"Still," Darcy said, "maybe you should have them meet *before* the *Teen Weekender* photographer comes to the reunion."

"Surprising them is what makes it so *dramatic*," Stephanie insisted. "And that's what Miss Stetson wants on the cover of *Teen Weekender*—high drama!"

Darcy sighed. "Stephanie, how come everything with you always has to be high drama?"

"I agree with Stephanie," Tamar said. "I think a surprise reunion makes for a much better story."

"Just what we need," Allie muttered. "*Two* headstrong Stephanies!"

"Twice the Tanner," Darcy added, "twice the *headaches!*"

Stephanie and Tamar smiled at each other.

"Trust me," Stephanie told her friends. "Everything will work out, and we'll be the first cousins ever to make the front page of *Teen Weekender!*"

CHAPTER
7

◆ ◀ ◢ ◆

"Can I ask you something?" Tamar asked later when she and Stephanie were locked in Stephanie's room planning the Tanner family reunion.

"Go ahead," Stephanie replied.

Tamar dabbed some red paint to fill in one of the Ns on the Tanner family reunion banner she was painting.

"Do you think what Allie said might be true? I mean, about our dads not being happy to see each other? They did have a big fight, after all. They might not ever want to see each other again."

Stephanie looked up from the cookbook she was reading and shook her head. "No way!" she said. "Think about it. Wouldn't *you* be happy to see a best friend after twenty years, no matter what kind of dumb fight you had?"

Tamar nodded. "I guess."

Stephanie went back to reading her cookbook. She was searching for a good pasta salad recipe to make for the reunion.

"Don't worry," she assured Tamar as she flipped through the pages. "I know my father. If there's one thing about him that's great, it's that he doesn't hold a grudge. Hey, his best friend Joey once stole his girlfriend—and Joey lives with us now!"

Tamar smiled. "Yeah, you're right. I'm just so eager for this whole thing to go smoothly. You know, so we can start being a *real* family."

"Me, too," Stephanie said. "Hey! Here's a good one—Greek chicken pasta salad."

"Sounds delicious," Tamar agreed. "I love Greek food."

"So do I!" Stephanie said. "Uncle Jesse makes the best Greek food. I wonder if I can get him to make spinach pies for the reunion."

"He knows about the reunion?" Tamar asked in surprise. "I thought he said we shouldn't—"

Stephanie held up her hand. "Relax!" she said. "I told him I ditched the reunion dinner plans. I also asked him not to tell Dad that I know about Ben. I promised Uncle Jesse I'd tell Dad myself."

"Good idea. But then, how are you going to get him to make spinach pie?" Tamar asked.

Stephanie held the pencil eraser to her chin and thought hard. "I have no idea," she said.

"While we're on the subject, how are we going to get our families to Hillside Park on Saturday for the reunion?" Tamar asked.

Stephanie tapped her chin with the pencil a few times. "I have no idea," she replied.

"Me, either." Tamar sighed. "This is just terrific. Two great minds . . . and not one great idea!"

There was a knock on Stephanie's door.

"Stephanie! It's me. Open up."

Stephanie gasped in horror. "It's D.J.!" she whispered.

"What should we do?" Tamar whispered back. "We can't let her know about the reunion plans, can we?"

"No," Stephanie said. "Let's hide everything."

"Steph?" D.J. called.

"Hold on, I'll be right there!" Stephanie shouted.

Frantically, she and Tamar shoved the cookbooks under Stephanie's bed. Then carefully, they slid the wet banner under Michelle's bed so D.J. wouldn't see it.

Stephanie unlocked the door and D.J. barged into the room. "Why did you lock the door?" she demanded.

"Uh, to keep Michelle out," Stephanie fibbed. "This is Tamar, my friend from school."

D.J. smiled at Tamar. "Nice to meet you. What's that on your face?"

Uh-oh, Stephanie thought. She glanced at Tamar—and saw a bright red paint splotch on her cheek.

Tamar shot Stephanie a panicked glance. "Um . . ."

"It smells like paint in here," D.J. added.

"Oh, that?" Stephanie said. "Right. Um, we were painting a . . . a birdhouse a little while ago."

Tamar coughed. Stephanie could tell she was trying not to laugh.

D.J. looked confused. "A birdhouse?" she asked.

"It's for a school project," Stephanie said with a gulp.

"Yeah," Tamar put in. "For, um, science class. We're studying wild animals and the ways humans domesticate them."

Stephanie felt herself getting the giggles. She and Tamar were certainly good at coming up with stories together.

"Oh," D.J. said. "Anyway, Stephanie, you have to water Mrs. Rowan's plants for me again."

Stephanie didn't hesitate for a minute. She shook her head firmly. "No way! I am *not* doing that again," she replied. "I spent all weekend watering those plants and feeding that fat cat. No way, Deej!"

"Oh, come on, Steph!" D.J. wailed. "Please? I really, *really* need your help. My schoolwork is piling up, and I just don't have the time. You have to help me out."

Stephanie remained firm. "No, D.J., I can't. It's too big a job. And that stupid cat gives me the creeps. Last time I was there, it—"

Tamar cleared her throat. "Um, can I talk to you for a sec, Stephanie?" she asked.

Stephanie stared at Tamar in surprise.

"It's *important!*" Tamar insisted.

Stephanie turned to D.J. "Hang on." She walked across the room to Tamar. "What is it?" she whispered.

"Take the job!" Tamar whispered back.

"But I—"

"Wait! Listen to me. Take the *whole* job from your sister. Tell her you'll water the plants and feed the monster until Mrs. Rowan comes back from her vacation. Then tell D.J. you want whatever money Mrs. Rowan is paying her. We can use it to pay for the reunion."

Stephanie considered what Tamar said. It wasn't a bad idea. Her cousin was right—the extra money would come in handy. She hadn't even thought about what this family reunion was going to cost. Or where she was going to get the money to pay for it.

"Okay, Deej, I'll do it," she announced.

D.J.'s eyes widened. "You will?"

"Yup! But I want the whole job. Not just for today . . . for the entire week. And I want to get paid double whatever you're getting paid from Mrs. Rowan—like you promised."

D.J. didn't hesitate. "Great! The job is yours. Only don't tell Mrs. Rowan because she left me in charge. I don't know if she'd like me passing the responsibility off on my little sister."

Stephanie clenched her jaw. *I'm fourteen!* she wanted to say. *Hardly a "little" sister!* Instead, she said, "Fine."

"Don't blow it, Stephanie," D.J. warned. "Mrs. Rowan is counting on me. And don't forget to feed the—"

"I know, I know! Don't forget to feed the furball! Okay. Just give me the keys."

D.J. handed the keys to Stephanie, then left. Stephanie and Tamar high-fived.

"That was a great idea," Stephanie told her cousin as they carefully pulled the banner out from under the bed. "I'm glad you thought of it."

"We're a good team," Tamar said.

Stephanie began flipping through the cookbook again. "I don't think there are any more good recipes in here," she said after a few minutes. "Aunt Becky has a great cookbook downstairs in the kitchen."

"Let's go get it," Tamar said.

"There's a recipe for blondies in it," Stephanie

added as they stood up. "We can make them the night before and they'll still be good."

"Yum!" Tamar said. "Hey, let's take the banner down to your basement to dry," she added.

The girls carefully lifted the banner and headed into the hallway. Stephanie glanced both ways, checking for any family member.

"Okay, the coast is clear," she said. "Let's go."

They started down the steps and were about halfway down, when the front door swung open.

"Everyone, I'm home!"

Stephanie froze. Then she spun around to Tamar.

"Quick! Get back upstairs!" she whispered frantically. "We have to hide this banner or everything will be ruined. My dad is home!"

CHAPTER
8

◆ ◀ ✦ ◆

Stephanie and Tamar raced back into the bedroom and slammed the door behind them.

"That was close!" Stephanie whispered. "If my father had seen you, he might have recognized you."

"You think?" Tamar asked.

Stephanie nodded. "Definitely. When I first saw your father's picture, I thought he looked familiar. It was only later that I realized it was because you look exactly like him. So if my dad sees you—"

"He'll know who I am."

"Right."

"So what are we going to do?" Tamar asked. "Can I sneak out the window?"

Stephanie shook her head. "No way. It's too dangerous.

"Stephanie? Michelle? Joey?" Danny called out as he climbed the stairs. *"Anyone home?"*

Stephanie had to think fast. She yanked open her closet doors and grabbed a red baseball cap and an old pair of sunglasses.

"Here," she said, tossing them to Tamar. "Put these on."

There was a knock at the door as Tamar quickly pulled the cap over her head.

"Steph? Michelle?" Danny called again.

"Yeah, Dad! Just a second!" Stephanie replied. When Tamar had the sunglasses on, the girls shoved the banner back under Michelle's bed.

Stephanie opened the door.

"Dad!" she exclaimed. "You're home!" She threw her arms around him and tried to turn him away from Tamar. "How was your trip? I missed you so much!"

Danny smiled. "I missed you, too." Then he frowned. "Steph, have you been painting in here?"

"Painting?" Stephanie asked.

"Yes. It smells like paint in here." Danny sniffed a few times, then gazed around the room.

"Hello," he said to Tamar.

"Oh, *that*," Stephanie said. "We were just painting something for class. Me and my friend T—*Tina*. From school."

Tamar smiled at Danny. "Hi, Mr. Tanner," she said, trying to disguise her voice.

"Hi, Tina," Danny replied. "You know, you look—"

Stephanie panicked and rushed to Tamar's side.

"She was just leaving!" she cried, interrupting her father and ushering Tamar from the room in a hurry. "See you tomorrow, Tina!" she said.

"Bye!" Tamar said in her disguised voice. She quickly fled down the steps.

"I was going to say your friend Tina looked—"

Oh, no! Stephanie thought. *He recognizes Tamar!*

Thinking quickly, she threw her arms around her father. "I just missed you so much!" she wailed dramatically, trying to keep her father from saying anything more about Tamar's looks. "I'm so glad you're back!"

Danny laughed. "Well, I missed you, too, sweetheart—all of you! Where is Michelle? I have some souvenirs for everybody."

Stephanie's eyes lit up. "What did you bring me?" she asked.

"Funny thing is, I brought you home a pair of sunglasses, the same as your friend Tina was wearing. By the way, Tina looked pretty silly wearing sunglasses indoors."

Stephanie breathed a sigh of relief. *So that was what Dad was going to say!*

"Um, she has to wear them," Stephanie explained. "She has a . . . problem with her eye. So where are the glasses?" she went on, trying to change the subject. "Did you bring me anything else?"

Danny didn't answer. He was too busy staring at something on Stephanie's desk.

"Where did you get this?" he asked.

Stephanie gasped when she saw what her father was looking at. It was the photograph of him and Ben!

"Oh, that?" she asked. Her voice was shaky. "I found that in the hall closet."

To Stephanie's horror, Danny crumpled the photo in his fist.

"Dad!" she cried. "What did you do that for?"

"It's just an old photo," Danny muttered. "I should have thrown it away years ago."

Stephanie was shocked by how weird her father was acting.

"Why did you crumple it up? I think you look so handsome in that picture."

Danny's expression remained grim. "If you don't mind, Stephanie, I don't want to talk about that picture."

Stephanie swallowed nervously. She couldn't resist asking her father about Ben. "Dad," she said, "I was just wondering who that was in the picture with you."

Danny glared at her. "I told you," he snapped angrily. "I don't want to talk about that picture! And I *especially* don't want to talk about *him!*"

"But, Dad—"

"It's none of your business, Stephanie!" Danny said. Then his tone changed. "Listen, sweetheart, the person in that picture isn't important. He's nobody. Okay?"

Stephanie gazed down at the floor. "Yeah, okay," she replied.

"I don't want to talk about it anymore, understand?"

Stephanie nodded.

Danny kissed her on the head, then headed for the door. He stopped next to Michelle's bed.

"Steph, what is that?" he asked, pointing to the floor.

Stephanie nearly choked. It was the banner sticking out from under Michelle's bed.

"Nothing!" she cried, rushing over to push it back.

Danny stepped in front of her and pulled the banner out from under the bed.

Oh, no, Stephanie thought. *I'm doomed!*

"Tanner family reunion?" he asked in confusion. "What's going on?"

Stephanie didn't know what to say. "Oh, you mean *that?*" she asked, forcing a smile. "That is just . . . it's only a . . ."

Think, Stephanie, think! she told herself.

She gave a loud sigh. "Okay, it's no use trying to hide it anymore," she said. "You caught me!"

"What are you talking about, Stephanie?"

Stephanie spoke quickly. "See, you were away for so long, and D.J.'s been working on campus so much, and everyone's been so busy, I wanted to make a special gourmet dinner to celebrate everybody being home tonight!"

Danny's expression softened. "A gourmet dinner? Really? But I was away for only a week," he reminded her.

"Well, it felt like much longer!" Stephanie said. "And I'm just so happy you're back!"

Danny gave her a hug. "Honey, that's so thoughtful of you," he said gently. "But, wow, a gourmet dinner! You really shouldn't have gone through so much trouble!"

Stephanie hugged her father tightly. "Don't be silly!" she said, her voice croaking slightly. "What's a little gourmet meal for the best dad in the whole world?"

"I'll go get cleaned up and unpacked," Danny told her. "And to tell you the truth, I *am* kind of hungry! A gourmet meal sounds like an amazing idea! I'll meet you down in the kitchen."

Stephanie managed a smile. "Great!" she called after him. "In the kitchen!"

When her father left, Stephanie threw herself

onto her bed. Her head hit something hard—the cookbook she had left on her pillow.

"Ow!" she muttered, rubbing her head. Then she lifted the book and opened it.

"Okay. Gourmet meal, gourmet meal," she said, skimming the pages. "How do I manage to get myself into these messes?"

CHAPTER
9

◆ ◀ ▸ ◆

"Oh, no! The plants!" Stephanie cried.

In a panic her head jerked up and her eyes opened wide. She blinked a few times and gazed around the classroom on Tuesday morning.

"Excuse me?" Miss Carter, the study hall teacher, asked.

Stephanie blinked again. *Oh, man! I must have fallen asleep.*

"Is everything okay?" Miss Carter asked.

Stephanie cleared her throat. "Uh, yes. I'm fine, Miss Carter. Sorry about that."

Stephanie leaned over her homework as her face

reddened. She knew the other kids must have been staring at her.

I can't believe I fell asleep! she thought. She had been dreaming about Mrs. Rowan's gigantic cat when she realized that she hadn't watered the plants or fed the cat Monday.

Of course, after cooking a huge last-minute dinner for nine people, and then cleaning up, she just hadn't had time. Unfortunately, she hadn't had time to do her math homework, either, and now she had wasted an entire study hall sleeping.

Stephanie rubbed her temples. Things were starting to really pile up. Planning the reunion with Tamar was taking up so much of her time that she was slacking off on her other responsibilities. She hadn't even started her science project on photosynthesis, which was due on Friday.

The reunion on Saturday would make it all worthwhile, she thought with a smile.

When study hall was over, Stephanie raced to her social studies classroom to meet with Miss Stetson. It was her lunch period, but Miss Stetson had specifically requested that Stephanie and Tamar meet with her.

I hope this meeting means what I think it means!

Stephanie thought excitedly. Maybe Miss Stetson had finally made up her mind about the *Teen Weekender* cover story. Stephanie crossed her fingers and stepped into the classroom.

Tamar was already there, and she was smiling.

Stephanie hurried over to her cousin. "What's going on?" she asked.

Miss Stetson stepped forward. "Stephanie," she said. "I have decided that the story of your father's reunion with his cousin is perfect for our cover story."

Stephanie's heart leapt. *Yes!* she silently cheered.

"Wow, that's great!" she said happily. Tamar squeezed her hand in excitement.

"I reviewed your idea with my editorial committee," Miss Stetson went on, "and we all agreed your story idea was the best. An article about the happy, joyous reunion of your fathers will make a great feature in our magazine."

"We think so, too," Tamar told her.

"Are your reunion plans all set?" Miss Stetson asked. "Because I don't want to show up with an expensive photographer if you don't have every last detail worked out."

Tamar opened her mouth to answer, but Stephanie beat her to it.

"Oh, don't worry about that!" Stephanie assured her. "We've got the entire reunion planned already."

She could feel Tamar staring at her.

"The food, the decorations—everything!" Stephanie added.

"Terrific!" Miss Stetson said. "So tell me—how are you going to get your fathers to the reunion without telling them where they're going?"

Stephanie heard Tamar gulp. The truth was, they hadn't a clue as how to get their families to Hillside Park.

"Oh, that was the easiest part," Stephanie fibbed. Tamar nodded in agreement.

"But we want it to be a surprise, of course," Stephanie added. "So we're not at liberty to disclose that information just yet."

Miss Stetson stared at her strangely. Then she opened her appointment book and made some notes.

"Then I guess I'll see you on Saturday," she said. "At Hillside Park. Noon sharp."

"See you then!" Stephanie replied. "Thanks, Miss Stetson."

"Oh, and remember—the deadline for the story is Monday morning," Miss Stetson called after them.

"No problem!" Stephanie called back.

In the hallway Stephanie felt like skipping. "How totally cool is this?" she asked. "Now it's official—we're going to be cover girls!"

Tamar gave her a half-smile. "I know it's cool," she said uneasily, "but I'm kind of worried."

Stephanie scrunched up her nose. "About what?" she asked.

"Well, you told Miss Stetson everything was set for the reunion—and it's not."

Stephanie rolled her eyes. "But it *will* be!" she insisted. "I had to tell her that so she wouldn't change her mind about giving us the cover story. I want her to think we have everything under control."

"But—"

"Tamar, stop worrying! By Saturday . . . we *will* have everything under control. It will be a piece of cake. Now, come on, let's get to the cafeteria. I need Allie to help me with my math homework."

In the cafeteria Allie and Darcy were already eating.

"Hey, guys!" Stephanie said, plopping down in the seat next to Darcy. "We did it! Miss Stetson just gave us the official word."

Tamar took a seat across the table from her. "We got the cover story," she announced.

Allie and Darcy both smiled. "That's great, you guys," Allie said.

"Cool!" Darcy added.

"Before we give you all the details, I need your help desperately, Allie."

Stephanie pulled out her math homework assignment.

"Can you help me with this?" she asked. "I didn't get to do it last night."

Allie made a face. "I don't want to do math during my only free period," she complained.

"Please?" Stephanie begged. "I have to hand it in next period."

Allie groaned. "Okay, but at least let me finish my lunch!"

"Yeah, okay," Stephanie said. She put down the homework assignment.

"How come you didn't do your homework yesterday?" Darcy asked her.

Stephanie sighed. "Tamar and I were working

on the family reunion," she explained. "And then I had to cook a gourmet meal for my father."

"What?" Darcy asked.

Stephanie groaned. "It's a long story," she said. "But I was up half the night cleaning the kitchen."

"No wonder you didn't have time to do your homework," Allie said.

Stephanie nodded. "Plus, I totally forgot to feed the neighbor's cat and water her plants," she added.

Tamar grimaced. "Yikes! What are you going to do?" she asked.

Stephanie sat back in her chair. "I'll go over there first thing after school today," she said.

"Oh! That reminds me!" Tamar said suddenly. "We should buy those T-shirts as soon as possible, so we have enough time to iron on all the names!"

"What T-shirts?" Darcy asked.

Stephanie took a bite of her sandwich. "Tamar had the best idea for the reunion," she said. "We're going to get T-shirts and iron on letters that say TANNER FAMILY REUNION on the front and everyone's name on the back."

"That sounds like a lot of work," Allie commented.

"It is," Tamar told her. "So we have to buy the shirts today so there's enough time to do them."

Stephanie exhaled loudly. "We absolutely have to go today?" she asked.

Tamar nodded. "Or they'll never be ready by Saturday."

Stephanie thought about the science project that she obviously wasn't going to get to that night, either. *Maybe I can work on it when I get home from shopping,* she thought. *Or at least after dinner.*

"Okay, I think I can get my father to drop me off at the mall tonight," she told Tamar. "Can you meet me there?"

"Yes. How about after dinner?"

"Okay. But I have to get back home early," Stephanie said. "I have a science project due this week and I haven't even started it."

As Stephanie unwrapped the sandwich she'd brought, Allie and Darcy were quiet.

"Stephanie," Allie said finally, breaking the silence. "Are you sure this reunion thing is really such a good idea? I mean, not the article idea, but the actual reunion?"

Stephanie glanced up. "What do you mean?

Of course it is," she said. "It's going to be amazing!"

Allie shook her head. "I don't know. It seems like a lot of work for something you're not even sure is going to turn out the way you expect. What if your plans backfire?"

"It *is* a lot of work," Stephanie said. "But it's all going to be worth it in the end! Our dads are going to make up and we're going to have an amazing day. Plus, we'll have a great story for the cover of *Teen Weekender!*"

"Yeah, but—"

"Allie," Stephanie interrupted, "didn't you have an awesome time at *your* family reunion?"

Allie nodded. "Yes, but—"

"Then stop worrying about my family reunion. It's going to be just as great! My father is going to be so happy to see Tamar's father . . . I just know it! And next Friday the whole world will get to read all about it when our story comes out in *Teen Weekender!*"

After dinner that night Stephanie's father drove her to the mall. Stephanie got nervous when he parked the car instead of dropping her off.

"Dad? What are you doing?" she asked.

"I need socks," Danny told her. "Since I'm here and all."

"Oh. Okay," Stephanie said. *How do I stop him?* she wondered frantically.

She walked through the mall doors. Her father followed her. He kept following her as she headed toward the T-shirt place, where she was meeting Tamar.

"I thought you said you had to buy socks," she said to Danny. "You need to go the other direction to get to that store with all the ties and socks. It's all the way on the other side of the mall."

Danny kept walking. "I don't like that store," he replied. "The socks are too expensive. I was going to go to Benson's Department Store instead."

Stephanie held her breath. Benson's was right next to the place where she was meeting Tamar!

Okay, don't panic, she told herself.

"Oh, that's a good idea," she said, trying to sound casual. "But wait! I just remembered the sock store is having a sale. A big sale—half off everything!"

"Really?" Danny said. He stopped walking.

"Then I guess I should go there instead." He glanced at his watch. "So how about we meet in forty-five minutes back at the entrance where we came in?"

Stephanie nodded eagerly. Forty-five minutes was all the time she needed to buy the T-shirts.

"Great! Okay! No prob—"

Stephanie nearly choked when she noticed Tamar right behind them, only two stores away! Their eyes met, and Tamar made a face. Then she pointed to the man walking with her.

It was *Ben!*

Oh, no! Stephanie froze. She couldn't let her father bump into Ben! Not here! Not now! Everything she and Tamar had worked so hard for would be ruined for sure.

What could she do? If her father turned around right now, he'd see Ben!

"Uh, no, wait!" Stephanie suddenly exclaimed. "On second thought, Dad, the sock store sale doesn't start until *Thursday*."

Danny groaned. "Are you sure, Stephanie?" he asked. "Maybe I should check it out—"

Stephanie pulled her father's arm and started walking quickly through the mall. "Positive!" she said. "I'm positive. And, anyway, I was thinking, why don't we ditch the shopping altogether?"

"Huh?" Danny asked in confusion.

"Let's get out of here!" Stephanie said. "I just remembered I already *have* the supplies I need for my science project at home."

"But I'd still like to get some socks—"

"Forget the socks!" Stephanie cried. "What about ice cream?"

"Ice cream?" Danny repeated.

"Yes, ice cream!" She threw her arms around her father and gave him a bear hug, at the same exact second Tamar and her father walked by. Stephanie spun her father around in the hug so he wouldn't see his cousin.

"We should spend some quality time together, Dad," she said. "Don't you agree?"

"Well, yes, but—"

"Okay! Then it's settled. Let's go to the food court for some Ben and Jerry's, okay? It'll give us a chance to talk and spend some father-daughter time."

Danny's eyes twinkled at the suggestion of Ben & Jerry's. "I guess some ice cream would be nice," he said.

"Great! Come on, Dad." She wanted to get as far away from Tamar and Ben as possible. And Ben & Jerry's was clear across the mall.

Stephanie's mind raced as they walked to Ben & Jerry's. This little ice cream side-trip was going to push her way off schedule. She'd never make it home in time to start her science project now. Unless she stayed up late again to work on it.

She grew tired just thinking about all the sleep she wasn't going to get tonight!

This will all be worth it in the end, Stephanie told herself. *This will all be worth it in the end. This will all be worth it in the end!*

No matter how many times she repeated it to herself, she still could hear Allie's voice over and over in her head.

"What if your plans backfire?" Allie had asked.

Stephanie pushed the thought away.

That's not going to happen, she told herself. *I won't let it happen.*

CHAPTER
10

◆ ◀ ◆ ◆

On Thursday evening when Stephanie had finished eating and was clearing away the dinner there was a knock at the Tanner's back door. Stephanie's hands were full, so Michelle answered the door.

"Hi!" she heard Michelle say. "Who are you?"

"Hi, uh, I'm Tina. Is Stephanie home?"

Stephanie recognized Tamar's voice and ran to the door the same time her father came in from the living room. Stephanie watched as Tamar quickly put on her sunglasses.

"Hi!" Stephanie said to Tamar. She noticed her cousin was carrying an overstuffed knapsack.

"Hi, Stephanie," Tamar said in her disguised voice. "Hello, Mr. Tanner."

"You know, you don't have to disguise your voice," Stephanie whispered in Tamar's ear. "My father doesn't know what you sound like!"

"Oh, right!" Tamar whispered back.

"Hi, Tina," Danny said. "How's your eye?"

Tamar seemed confused. Stephanie made a face at her as if to say, I had to think of *something* to explain the dark sunglasses!

"Oh, my eye, right. It's fine," Tamar replied uneasily.

"Come on, let's go up to my room," Stephanie said quickly.

"Steph, I thought you were going to finish your science project right after dinner," Danny reminded her. "It's due tomorrow."

Stephanie stopped halfway up the stairs. "I am," she told her father. "Uh, Tina is helping me with the project. She's a science whiz, you know!"

Tamar stood behind Stephanie on the steps and nodded.

"Really?" Danny asked.

"Science is my best subject," Tamar told him.

"Okay then," Danny said. "If you two need

help, give a yell." Danny poured himself a cup of coffee and headed back into the living room.

Stephanie and Tamar continued upstairs. "Michelle!" Stephanie called back down to her sister. "We'd like a little privacy, okay?"

"Okay," Michelle replied. "But why is Tina wearing sunglasses in the house?" she asked.

"Never mind," Stephanie told her.

In Stephanie's room, Tamar flung the knapsack onto Stephanie's bed and unzipped it.

"I bought enough T-shirts for everybody!" she said excitedly. "Look at how great they came out!" She held up a bright green T-shirt that Tamar had already printed:

TANNER FAMILY REUNION

HILLSIDE PARK

Stephanie squealed with delight and pulled it over her head.

"I love it!" she cried. "I'm so happy you were able to get them today. It's such a relief after Tuesday night's big washout at the mall!"

Tamar tried one of the shirts on, too. "I know! That was so close. I thought they'd see each other for sure."

Stephanie reached under her bed and pulled

out an iron and an ironing board. "This is going to be so cool! Did you get the iron-on letters?"

Tamar nodded and pulled a bag of iron-on letters from the knapsack.

"We should start ironing right away because it's going to take a while. Plus, each shirt has to cool off and set before we can fold it up."

Stephanie frowned. "Really? How long do you think it will take?" she asked. "Because I *really* have to finish my science project tonight. I've been putting everything off lately to do reunion stuff."

"I know. Me, too," Tamar said. "Plus, I have to make up a million excuses to get out of my house on school nights. At least my brother is being nice about driving me here. I think he's just happy he gets to borrow Dad's car."

"Our families are going to be so surprised," Stephanie said excitedly. "Nobody expects a thing. Just imagine their faces when we introduce ourselves as cousins on Saturday!"

Tamar smiled. "They're going to be so happy. Especially our fathers. My dad gets pretty weepy at family things—he's really a big sap sometimes."

"My dad, too!" Stephanie said. "Maybe that's why they were so close," she added. "They were so much alike."

"Like us," Tamar said.

"Exactly!"

The girls began ironing the letters on the back of each T-shirt, spelling out each family member's name. Stephanie even made a T-shirt for Joey, who was practically a Tanner anyway.

"So I thought of a good way to get everybody to the park on Saturday," Stephanie said as they ironed.

"Yeah? What is it?" Tamar asked.

"Well, I heard there's a big antique and collectibles fair at the park on the same day," Stephanie said. "Joey's been looking all over for an old comic book for his collection, so I thought I'd suggest that we all go together and help him look. My dad loves antiques and my uncle and aunt can bring the kids because there'll be rides there."

"Wow, Steph! That's great thinking."

"We'll just have to think of a way to get them over to the picnic area at the park. You and I will have to go earlier to set everything up, of course."

Tamar nodded. "It sounds like it just might work out after all!" she exclaimed.

"You bet it will. And I'll call Miss Stetson tomorrow and confirm everything."

Tamar clasped her hands together in excitement. "I can't believe that a week from tomorrow our story is going to be on the cover of *Teen Weekender!*"

"I know, isn't it amazing?" Stephanie asked. "But we've earned it," she added. "I've been putting off so many things in order to get ready for the family reunion."

"Tell me about it," Tamar agreed.

"Whoops!" Stephanie said suddenly. "That reminds me—I've *got* to get over to Mrs. Rowan's house! I managed to feed her cat yesterday, but I've missed two days of watering her plants! If the plants die, D.J. will kill me."

"Okay. I'd better get going anyway. We can finish the shirts tomorrow night, after we fix all the food."

Stephanie nodded. "I took care of everything for tomorrow night," she told Tamar. "My father and Joey are taking Michelle to a movie, and my aunt and uncle are visiting relatives. We'll have the whole house to ourselves!"

"Excellent!"

"But we'd better take these shirts to the basement to cool off. I don't want Michelle to find them in our room," Stephanie added. "And then I *have* to get cracking on my science project. I barely even remember what photosynthesis is."

Stephanie and Tamar slipped down to the kitchen and then tiptoed down the basement steps.

"A few of these aren't cooled and haven't set yet," Tamar said. "What should we do with them?"

Stephanie thought for a minute. "We'll just have to lay them out," she said. "Nobody ever comes down here anyway—it's such a mess. So no one will see them."

They left the shirts to cool and headed back upstairs.

After Tamar's brother came by to pick her up, Stephanie raced over to Mrs. Rowan's house. It took at least ten minutes to find the cat, who was hiding. Then she quickly fed him and watered as many of the plants as she could.

I'll have to do the rest tomorrow, she told herself. *If I don't do my science project right now, I'll never have it done for tomorrow.*

Stephanie locked up the neighbor's house and ran back home. *Finally I can get some work done*, she thought as she hurried through the kitchen.

"Hi, Steph," Danny said, walking into the kitchen and heading straight for the basement door.

"Dad!" Stephanie yelled as her father turned the doorknob.

Danny spun around, startled. "What? Stephanie, what is it?" he asked.

"Sorry, Dad, I didn't mean to scream," Stephanie told him in a calmer voice. "It's just . . . well, I was wondering where you were going."

"I was just going down to the basement," Danny told her. "You scared me, you know."

"Sorry," Stephanie said again. "But what do you want to go down there for? It's a mess!"

"I know it's a mess, Stephanie. That's why I'm carrying all these cleaning products." He held up about three spray bottles. "Because I'm planning to *clean up* the mess!"

Stephanie didn't know what to do. She couldn't let her father go downstairs . . . the reunion T-shirts were lying out in the open!

There was only one thing to do.

"I'll clean the basement," she offered, trying to sound more excited about it than she felt.

"That's okay, I don't mind—"

"No, Dad. Really. Let me do it. I was heading down there anyway to look for something for my science project. So I might as well clean while I'm there."

"Are you sure you have time?" Danny asked.

Oh, yeah, tons of time! Stephanie thought sarcastically. *So what if my science project is sitting upstairs, half finished? So what if I haven't done any math homework all week?*

"Sure," she said out loud, taking the bottles away from her father.

"Well, thanks, Steph," Danny said. "It's nice of you to volunteer!"

Stephanie sighed. She knew she was looking at another late night of schoolwork and very little sleep. Cleaning the basement was going to take forever.

"My pleasure," she said, trying to sound as cheery as she could.

It'll all be worth it in the end! she reminded herself.

And at least *now* the end was only a day away!

CHAPTER
11

◆ ◀ ✦ ◆

Stephanie stretched a large green tablecloth over the wooden picnic table at the park and secured each corner with a heavy rock.

Tamar showed up just as she was finished covering the third table.

"Stephanie, this place looks incredible!" Tamar exclaimed. "I can't believe you found green tablecloths to match the T-shirts."

Stephanie stood back from the tables and gazed around the picnic area. She grinned proudly.

"It *does* look awesome," she said. There were

green streamers hanging from all the trees, and she had decorated all the sandwich platters she and Tamar had spent making the night before.

"What did you tell your family?" Stephanie asked Tamar.

Tamar smiled. "I told them I was trying out for a softball team, and that I needed them to come to the park at noon to cheer me on."

Stephanie nodded. "I'm impressed, cousin!" she said. "That was a great idea!"

"What did you tell your family?" Tamar asked.

"Well, I told them I had to come to the collectibles fair early to meet Allie, and that I would meet them all in the picnic area at noon. Then Allie told her father about the reunion, and he thought it was a great idea, so he helped me load all the stuff into his car and drove me here."

"Cool," Tamar said. "This is so exciting!" she added. "I can't believe the big day is finally here. How do I look?"

Both girls were wearing their Tanner Family Reunion T-shirts, and Tamar had put a matching green headband in her hair.

"Great! I love the headband," Stephanie told her.

Tamar pulled another one from her Sport-Glo pack. "I brought one for you, too."

"Thanks." Stephanie put it in her hair exactly as Tamar had, and the cousins looked as similar as they did on the first day they met.

Stephanie checked her watch. It was 11:45. The only thing left to do was hang the banner.

As Stephanie and Tamar hung the Tanner Family Reunion sign between two trees, Miss Stetson and the photographer from *Teen Weekender* arrived.

The photographer started taking pictures of Stephanie and Tamar getting ready for the big reunion.

"This is some story," Miss Stetson told Stephanie. "If you can pull it off, that is."

"Oh, don't worry about that!" Stephanie assured her. "It's going to be a real tear-jerker here in a few minutes!"

"And both your fathers *really* don't know anything about this?" Miss Stetson asked.

"Nope," Tamar replied. "Our dads haven't spoken to each other in twenty years!"

"How about a picture of both of you under the banner?" the photographer asked. "For the cover."

Stephanie and Tamar grinned at each other.

It was really happening! Stephanie thought she would pass out from excitement.

The girls posed together, hugging and standing under the Tanner Family Reunion banner.

"Got it," the photographer called out. "And it looks like some more of your party has arrived."

Stephanie spun around to see her family's minivan pulling up to the picnic area.

"It's my dad! My family is here!" Stephanie cried.

Stephanie, Tamar, and Miss Stetson watched as Danny, Michelle, D.J., Uncle Jesse, Aunt Becky, the twins, and Joey stepped out of the minivan. They began walking toward the picnic tables.

"They didn't even notice the decorations yet," Tamar said, smiling.

Stephanie waved. "Dad! Over here!" she called out. Next to her, the photographer began snapping away.

Her father seemed totally confused as he approached the picnic area.

"Here we go," Stephanie whispered to Tamar.

"And here comes *my* family," Tamar whispered back.

Stephanie gazed past her family and saw Tamar's parents and her two brothers climbing out of their car.

"Stephanie," Danny asked as he gazed up at the banner, "what's going on?"

"Steph, you didn't have to go to so much trouble for a comic book fair," Joey joked, pointing to the picnic table filled with food. "I would have settled for a hot dog and a soda at the snack bar."

"What's all this for?" Danny asked again. "And what does your T-shirt say?"

Uncle Jesse was staring at her with a strange expression on his face. He glanced around at all the decorations. Then his gaze fell on Ben, who was moving toward them.

"Oh, no, Stephanie. Tell me you *didn't* do this!" Jesse cried.

"Do what?" Danny asked. "Stephanie! Can you please tell me what this is all about?"

"Okay," Stephanie said finally. "Dad, we've been planning this surprise for you all week."

The photographer moved closer to Danny and kept taking pictures. Danny glanced over at him and frowned. "Will you excuse us, please?" he asked.

The photographer moved a few steps back but kept snapping pictures.

"Steph?" Danny asked in confusion.

"Welcome to the Tanner family reunion!" Stephanie told him.

"But—" Danny began.

"Cool! Blondies!" Nicky yelled, speeding between Stephanie and her father. He and Alex practically attacked the picnic table.

"Boys!" Becky cried, running after them. "No dessert until you've eaten lunch!"

"Stephanie—" Danny began again.

"All right! Blondies!" yelled a little blond kid. He ran right in front of Danny, heading for the picnic table. Stephanie guessed he was Tamar's little brother.

"Stephen," Tamar's mother called, following her son. "No sweet stuff yet."

Stephanie glanced over at the picnic table—and grinned. All three little boys were stuffing their faces with blondies as they tried to hide from their moms. Becky and Tamar's mother began chasing them around, trying to get the blondies away. Everyone was laughing—it was like a big game of tag.

This is exactly the way I imagined it, Stephanie thought. *We're a family!*

"The kids have made friends already," Tamar cried, hurrying over to Stephanie. "Can you get some pictures of that?" she asked the photographer.

"Good idea," he said, turning toward the picnic table. Michelle rushed over and joined in the game, mugging for the camera.

"*Stephanie!*" Danny yelled.

Stephanie jumped and spun around.

"What is going on here?" he demanded. "Who is this photographer? What is this all about?"

Stephanie looked over her father's shoulder. Ben was crossing the grass, gazing in surprise at the decorations.

It was time for the main event. Stephanie grinned at Tamar and reached for her cousin's hand.

"This is a family reunion," she announced. "And say hello to somebody you haven't seen in twenty years—your cousin, *Ben Tanner!*"

Stephanie took her father's arm and turned him around so he was face to face with Tamar's dad.

Danny's eyes widened as he and Ben stared at each other in total disbelief. The *Teen Weekender* photographer circled them, snapping pictures rapidly.

Stephanie kept her eyes focused on her father's face. She watched as he stared at Ben in amazement. Her heart was beating like crazy.

She squeezed Tamar's hand. "Look how surprised they are!" she whispered. "Do you think they'll hug?"

"If they do, I hope the photographer gets a great shot!" Tamar replied. She squeezed Stephanie's hand, too.

Then Stephanie saw her father's expression change. He didn't look surprised. Or happy. Or like he wanted to do any hugging.

He looked *angry.*

Danny finally spoke. "What are *you* doing here?" he demanded. His voice was shaking.

Ben's expression had changed, too. He gazed straight at Tamar. "Did you know *he* was going to be here?"

Tamar nodded. "Of course, Dad," she said. "Stephanie and I found out about each other at school and we started planning this surprise reunion."

Stephanie stepped up to the two cousins. "See,

Dad?" she said. "Tamar and I were so lucky to find each other, and we wanted you and Ben to work everything out so we could all be a family again."

"A family?" D.J. cut in. "What do you mean?"

"It's the coolest thing," Stephanie told her sister. "Tamar's father is Dad's cousin. Tamar and her brothers are our second cousins!"

"Wow!" D.J. cried. "That's amazing."

"I never knew we had any cousins in San Francisco," said Brian, Tamar's older brother.

"And now—" Stephanie started to say.

"Stephanie!" Danny bellowed.

She glanced at her father. His face was beet red. He had folded his arms across his chest and was gazing angrily at Stephanie. "How could you do this?" he asked.

Stephanie swallowed nervously. Her father looked as though he might explode.

"You're in big trouble, Stephanie Tanner!"

CHAPTER
12

◆　◀　✦　◆

"Stephanie, how could you do this?" Danny demanded.

Everyone fell silent. Stephanie could feel Tamar trembling beside her.

"I—I—I thought you would want to see each other after all these years," Stephanie said quietly. "Especially since you were so close."

"I have nothing to say to *him!*" Danny snapped.

"Well, *I* have nothing to say to you either!" Ben chimed in just as angrily.

"Dad," Stephanie began, "can't you at least talk

things over with Ben? Whatever happened was a long time ago—"

"Stephanie, you don't know the first thing about what B—*he* did to me! If you did, you would understand why I never want to see him again!"

Ben stepped up to Danny and shook a finger in his cousin's face. "What *I* did?" he shouted. "You have it all wrong! *You* were the one responsible for—"

"*Me?*" Danny yelled. "No! *You're* the one who—"

"Dad!" Stephanie cried, trying to step between her father and Ben. "Please! Don't fight!"

"If you hadn't been so irresponsible!" Danny shouted at Ben.

"That's not the way *I* remember it!" Ben yelled back.

Tamar joined Stephanie between their fathers. "Dad! Please. Stephanie's right. You shouldn't fight. You weren't supposed to fight today."

"Oh, just forget it," Danny said angrily. He spun around and stormed back toward the mini-van. "Let's go," he called to the others.

Nobody moved.

"I said, let's go!" Danny yelled.

Uncle Jesse hurried over to the twins. "Come on, boys," he said quickly. "It's time to leave."

"No!" Alex wailed. "We're playing!"

"We're having fun with Stephen," Nicky cried.

"Uncle Danny wants to go home now," Becky told them.

"No!" Alex said again. Nicky burst into tears.

Uncle Jesse picked him up and started walking toward the van. "I wanna play with Stephen!" Nicky sobbed.

Becky gave Stephanie a helpless look. "Maybe you can play with Stephen some other day," she told the twins.

"They are family," Jesse added, giving Danny a serious look.

"I don't care," Danny growled. "Right now, we're getting as far away from *him* as possible. Come on, Michelle!" he added.

Michelle slowly walked over to the minivan.

"Dad! Wait!' Stephanie called.

Danny spun around. "I have nothing to say to you, Stephanie," he said quietly. "I'm so angry right now that it's best if I don't talk to you at all."

Stephanie's face felt hot. She'd never seen her father like this before.

What have I done?

She wanted to cry as Danny turned his back on her and stalked over to the minivan.

"Tamar, I'm sorry about all this," D.J. said quickly. "But no matter what our fathers say, we're still cousins. We'll get together some other time and get to know each other."

"Deej!" Danny called.

D.J. hurried across the grass to the minivan. Stephanie could hardly breathe as she watched her family drive away.

"I don't know why you would do something like this to me," Ben said to Tamar. "But I'm too angry to even discuss it!"

"But, Dad—" Tamar began, her voice shaking.

"We'll talk later," Ben cut in. "For now, you clean up this mess. Come on, boys."

Stephen and Brian followed Ben to the car. Tamar's mother gave the two girls a sad smile. "Try not to worry too much," she told Tamar. "He and Danny will both calm down soon."

She got into the car and Tamar's family drove away, too.

"I can't believe what a disaster that was," Tamar murmured.

"Me either." Suddenly, Stephanie remembered the *Teen Weekender* article!

She turned to see Miss Stetson and the photographer packing up their equipment.

"Miss Stetson! Wait!" she cried. "Don't leave!"

Miss Stetson slung her bag over her shoulder. "There's no story here," she told the girls. "I'm disappointed in both of you," she added. "You led me to believe there was going to be a happy reunion here today—not a war. I trusted you."

"But I can explain—" Stephanie began.

Miss Stetson shook her head. "I don't think so," she said. "No reunion, no cover story."

Stephanie hung her head.

"We never expected this to happen," Tamar blurted out. "Our fathers were supposed to hug and be happy to see each other! This was supposed to be a big, happy family reunion. We made T-shirts and everything. Right, Steph?"

Stephanie didn't answer. She was thinking about how she had let everybody down—her father, Miss Stetson, even Tamar. She should have told her cousin about her father's reaction when he saw the photograph the other night.

She should have known Danny wouldn't be happy to see his long-lost cousin.

She had just told herself not to think about it—that everything would work out in the end.

Boy was I wrong, she thought sadly.

Stephanie and Tamar took a bus back to Stephanie's house. When they arrived, the house was empty.

Upstairs, Stephanie fell onto her bed and punched her pillow. "I can't believe we were so stupid to think it would work," she said.

"Tell me about it!" Tamar added, lying next to her cousin on the bed. "We were idiots! We should have listened to Allie and Darcy."

"All that planning!" Stephanie cried. "I didn't hand in my science project on Friday because of the reunion, and I'm going to lose ten points for lateness!"

"I didn't do my math homework for three days!" Tamar added, "so I could run back and forth to the mall and buy all those dumb shirts!"

"Yeah, and what about all the money we

wasted?" Stephanie pointed out. "All my allowance was spent on that food and on the decorations! Not to mention all the money I made—*Oh, no!*" She suddenly bolted off the bed.

"What?" Tamar asked. "What is it?"

"The plants!" Stephanie cried. "I totally forgot to go back and water the plants yesterday!"

"You're kidding!" Tamar groaned.

"No! Come on, we have to go over there!"

Stephanie raced downstairs and out the door. Tamar followed her to Mrs. Rowan's house. After struggling with the front door lock, Stephanie finally got inside. She rushed to check on the plants and to her surprise, their soil was damp.

Stephanie shrugged. "I guess the last watering was a good one," she said. "I should water the roses outside though," she added.

Tamar followed her into the kitchen. Stephanie stopped short when she noticed the cat's food dish was full.

Stephanie's heart skipped a beat. *"Full?* But how could that be? She always gobbles that stuff up the second I put it down."

Tamar frowned. "So why didn't she eat it this time?"

Stephanie gasped. "Oh, no. Maybe she's sick. I'd better find her."

She and her cousin stared at each other for a second. Then they both sprang into action.

"Here, Kitty!" Stephanie shouted. "Here Kitty, Kitty!"

She searched the downstairs, but the cat was nowhere to be found. "Where is that dumb cat?" Stephanie shouted as she stomped from room to room.

Then she had an awful thought. Her hand flew up to cover her mouth.

"What?" Tamar asked worriedly. "What's the matter?"

Stephanie lowered her hand. "I think," she said quietly, "that maybe—just *maybe*—the cat escaped when I was here the other day!"

Tamar's eyes widened. "You mean it got out?"

Stephanie nodded. "Yes. D.J. said to be careful because it likes to sneak out. I don't remember if I was careful!"

"How could you not be careful?" Tamar asked.

"I didn't *mean* to let it out," Stephanie snapped. "It was an accident!"

"Yeah, but if your sister *warned* you that the cat

likes to sneak out, I would think you'd be extra careful every time you opened the door."

Stephanie glared at her cousin. "I *was* careful," she insisted. "And this is all *your* fault anyway!"

"My fault?" Tamar demanded. "Are you nuts?"

"No, I'm not nuts!' Stephanie said. "You're the one who made me take this stupid job in the first place."

"So what if I did? *I* wasn't the dope who let the cat escape," Tamar cried.

"I'm not a dope!" Stephanie shouted.

"Well, you're obviously very irresponsible!" Tamar shouted back.

"I am not!" Stephanie insisted. "*You* are! And you have the worst ideas! I should never have listened to you about the reunion. It was the worst idea ever. And now my father's not speaking to me—because of *you!*"

Tamar put her hands on her hips. "Fine—think what you want to think! But cousin or not, I'm not hanging around with you another second."

She spun around and stormed out the front door.

"Go!" Stephanie shouted after her. "I don't need another relative anyway!"

She watched Tamar stomp down the block and turn the corner. With a sigh Stephanie fell into Mrs. Rowan's porch swing.

Her father was mad at her.

Tamar was mad at her.

She'd lost the neighbor's cat—and now D.J. would probably be mad at her, too.

Yesterday her life had been great. She had a new cousin and a new best friend, and she was about to do something really amazing for her father.

Now everything was ruined.

It was all her fault.

CHAPTER
13

◆ ◀ ✦ ◆

Stephanie pushed open the back door and stepped into the kitchen. The house was still quiet.

I wonder where everyone is, she thought as she pulled open the refrigerator door. She took out some lemonade, poured herself a tall glass, and sat down at the kitchen table. She took a sip, then put the glass down and rubbed her sore legs. She'd been running all over the neighborhood for the past two hours looking for Mrs. Rowan's cat.

Unfortunately, she hadn't found it.

Stephanie sighed and put her head down on the

table. She was in the worst mood ever. With good reason, too, she figured. It wasn't every day a girl lost her dad, her best friend, and the neighbor's cat all in one afternoon.

Just then the back door opened and D.J. walked inside. "Stephanie!" she said. "I've been looking all over for you!"

"Where is everyone?" Stephanie asked.

"Uncle Jesse and Aunt Becky took the twins for ice cream, because they wouldn't stop crying about leaving the reunion, and Joey and Michelle tagged along."

"Where's Dad?" Stephanie asked.

"I'm not sure," D.J. said gently. "He wanted to be alone. Where were *you?*"

"I was watering the plants," Stephanie told her, leaving out the part about losing the cat. She wasn't ready to tell her sister the bad news just yet.

"You look awful," D.J. said, sitting in the chair next to her. "You must be totally bummed about the reunion, huh?"

Stephanie nodded. "You know, I thought I was doing this really great thing. I thought Dad would be so happy! He's always complaining that all his relatives live so far away, and here I found his long-lost cousin just a few blocks from us. It seemed like the perfect plan!"

D.J. was sympathetic. "I thought it was a great plan," she said. "If that makes you feel any better."

Stephanie nodded. "Yeah, it does, I guess."

"And who knows? Maybe Dad will come around," D.J. added. "If anything, he'll realize your intentions were good. Whether or not he wants to make up with Ben, he'll figure out that you were only trying to get the family back together."

Stephanie gazed at her older sister. Why had she been so mad at D.J. for the past week? Suddenly Stephanie felt angry with herself. D.J. hadn't been trying to take advantage of her—she'd been in a bind and needed help.

That's what sisters were for, anyway—to help each other out.

"Thanks, Deej," Stephanie said.

D.J. smiled. "So what happened with Tamar?" she asked. Stephanie frowned. "We took a bus back here, but then we kind of had a fight and now we're not speaking."

"Are you serious?" D.J. asked.

Stephanie nodded.

"What was the fight about?" D.J. asked.

Stephanie didn't want to bring up the lost cat yet, so instead she replied, "Over something silly."

"Well, it just so happens that on the way home from the park, Dad told us why he and Ben had that fight years ago."

"He did?" Stephanie asked.

D.J. nodded.

"Tell me!" Stephanie pleaded. "Tamar and I were wondering all this time what could have happened that would make them so mad at each other!"

"You won't believe it," D.J. told her.

"Tell me!" Stephanie said again.

"Okay—here it goes," D.J. began. "A few weeks before their high school graduation, there was a contest for all the students to write a speech for graduation."

Stephanie nodded.

"Dad says he told Ben about a great idea he had for a speech," D.J. went on. "It took him two weeks to write it, then he ended up changing his mind and writing another speech.

"So Ben asked if he could use Dad's first idea for his own speech and Dad said okay. But then, the night before graduation, Dad learned Ben's speech had been picked—Ben was going to read his speech at graduation."

"Wasn't Dad happy for Ben?" Stephanie asked.

"Yes. At first he was. Then, at graduation, Dad flipped out because Ben used Dad's old speech—word for word!"

Stephanie's eyes widened. "I can't believe it. You mean Ben *stole* Dad's speech?"

"It looks that way," D.J. said.

"But Dad had written another speech anyway," Stephanie pointed out.

"I know," D.J. said. "But Dad was still furious, and he never forgave Ben for winning with his speech."

"And *that's* why they never spoke again?" Stephanie asked.

D.J. nodded. "One thing led to another, and they stopped talking, then Ben moved away, and they never bothered to make up."

Stephanie sat back in her chair. "Wow," she said.

"Yeah, it's a pretty outrageous story," D.J. said.

"So what was your fight with Tamar about anyway?" she asked.

Stephanie remembered the cat and got a sick feeling in her stomach. She knew it was time to tell D.J. the truth.

"D.J., listen," she began, "I, um, accidentally let Mrs. Rowan's cat out a few days ago, and it's gone. I was over there before and I couldn't find it anywhere. I searched the entire neighborhood." She braced herself for D.J.'s reaction. "I'm so sorry, D.J.!" she added.

To Stephanie's surprise, D.J. started laughing.

"What's so funny?" Stephanie asked. "Didn't you hear me? I said the cat is *missing!*"

"No, it's not!" D.J. told her. "Chrysanthemum is *here!*"

"Chrysanthemum?" Stephanie asked.

"Chrissy. The cat," D.J. said. "I went over to Mrs. Rowan's this morning, figuring you might need some help watering all the plants. Chrissy looked lonely, so I brought her back here with me. She's up in my room right now."

Stephanie breathed a sigh of relief. "I can't believe it," she cried. "I thought that cat was history!"

"Nope. She's fine. And by the way, here's the

money I owe you for taking care of her and the plants." D.J. handed her twenty dollars.

Stephanie gave her back the money. "Never mind the money," she told her sister. "I was doing you a favor."

"Really? Why?" D.J. asked.

"Because we'll always be there for each other. No matter what," Stephanie said. "That's what family is for."

"I have some bad news, class," Mr. Leviton announced on Monday. "It's about *Teen Weekender.*"

Stephanie slid down lower in her desk chair as Allie and Darcy both turned to look at her.

"What's he talking about?" Allie whispered.

Stephanie shrugged. She hadn't called either of her best friends yesterday to tell them about the reunion. Since her dad was still so mad at her, she had spent most of the day in her room. "Well . . ." she began.

"As you know, today was the deadline for stories submitted to the magazine," the teacher went on. "And unfortunately our class story is not written. We've missed the deadline."

Stephanie heard groans of disappointment from the other kids. A few of them shot her questioning glances. She felt her cheeks grow warm.

"Steph?" Allie asked. "What happened? Why didn't you and Tamar write the story?"

Stephanie gazed at her cousin. Tamar was staring down at her desk, embarrassed. She didn't even glance in Stephanie's direction.

"We had a fight," Stephanie told Allie. "The reunion was a huge disaster, and then Tamar blamed the whole thing on me."

"That doesn't sound like Tamar," Darcy put in. "Are you sure it wasn't just a misunderstanding?"

"No," Stephanie replied. "I never should have agreed to work with her in the first place. If I'd written a story by myself, this never would have happened."

Darcy and Allie exchanged worried looks. Stephanie bit her lip. She knew she wasn't being fair to Tamar, but she still felt so angry that she just didn't care.

Mr. Leviton didn't say anything more about the *Teen Weekender*, but Stephanie couldn't think of anything but the story. She had let everyone down, and she couldn't blame that on Tamar.

After class Stephanie grabbed her books and hurried out of the room. She didn't want to run into her cousin.

"Steph! Wait up," Darcy called behind her.

Stephanie turned around to see Allie and Darcy following her down the hall. Tamar was right next to them!

"You two are going to tell us what happened right now," Allie announced.

"We had a fight," Tamar mumbled, not looking at Stephanie. "The reunion was a terrible idea, and there's no way we could write about it. Now the whole class is mad at us."

"Well, it was *your* idea to write a story together," Stephanie snapped.

"But I'm not the one who came up with the idea for the reunion," Tamar said. "You should have known your dad would get upset."

"Well, *you* should have known *your* dad would be mad!" Stephanie cried.

"Hold on!" Allie said. "I can't believe you two."

"What do you mean?" Stephanie asked.

"You're acting just like your fathers," Allie explained. "They had a big fight, and now you two are fighting."

120

"Yeah," Darcy put in. "Is that how you want things to end? Two cousins drifting apart over a dumb fight, and then never bothering to make up?"

Stephanie looked at Tamar. She had been so happy to discover that she had a cousin, and now she had lost her. Stephanie tried to imagine what it would be like never to speak to Tamar again. It would be awful, she decided.

Slowly, Tamar began to smile. Stephanie smiled back.

"You're right," she told Darcy. "We're being just as stubborn as Dad and Ben!"

"Like fathers, like daughters," Tamar said with a laugh.

"I know you're mad at me for saying all those nasty things on Saturday," Stephanie told her, "but I'm sorry. Really! I was angry and I totally took it out on you."

"I guess I said some pretty horrible things, too," Tamar admitted.

"Well, I didn't mean a single word of it," Stephanie went on. "I don't want us to fight," she added. "I want us to be best cousins forever."

"Me, too!" Tamar confessed. "I was so upset when we had that fight."

"So was I! And just because our fathers are being stubborn over something that happened a long time ago, that doesn't mean we have to be like them."

"Right!"

"So what do you think?" Stephanie asked. "Are we friends again?"

"Definitely!" Tamar said. "We'll be cousins forever," she added, "that's the easy part. But we'll always have to *work* at being friends."

"Okay, cuz," Stephanie said, "now what do we do about our other problem?"

"You mean, how are you going to face everybody at school now that you aren't going to be on the cover of *Teen Weekender?*" Darcy asked.

"Exactly," Stephanie replied.

"I have no idea," Tamar said.

"Hey! Wait a minute!" Stephanie said slowly. "What was that you just said?"

"I said, I have no idea," Tamar repeated.

"No! About us being cousins and having to work at being friends."

"Yes, that's what I said."

"Well, you just gave me a great idea!" Stephanie exclaimed.

"What is it?" Tamar asked.

Stephanie was so excited she could hardly get the idea out. "Okay, so our first story idea was a total washout. But what if we went to Miss Stetson and told her we have an even *better* story?"

"Do we have a better story?" Tamar asked.

Stephanie grinned. "We sure do!" she exclaimed. "How about the story of two long-lost cousins who are struggling to stay together and remain friends despite a twenty-year family feud?"

"Steph, that's a great idea!" Allie cried.

"It's not just great," Tamar said. "It's *brilliant!*"

"But it's too late," Darcy pointed out. "You already missed the deadline."

Stephanie frowned. Darcy was right. But now they had the perfect story idea! There had to be some way to get it into the magazine.

"Maybe we can write the story at lunchtime," Tamar suggested. "If we get it done then, we can still make the deadline."

"Do you think Miss Stetson will let you hand it in at the end of the day instead of the beginning?" Allie asked.

"There's only one way to find out!" Stephanie said. "Come on, cuz. Let's go find Miss Stetson."

CHAPTER
14

◆ ◀ ✦ ◆

"I can't believe the week I've had," Stephanie murmured on Friday evening.

She had been working nonstop ever since Monday, trying to catch up on all the homework she'd missed while she was planning the family reunion with Tamar.

It was all worth it, though, she thought happily. Miss Stetson had agreed to give the girls until five on Monday to turn in their story. When they did, she had read it on the spot and declared it one of the best student-written pieces she'd ever seen.

If only our story could have had a happier ending

for our fathers, Stephanie thought as she wandered down the stairs to get a snack. *Tamar and I are such great friends—it stinks that Dad and Ben will never be friends again.*

The worst part was that Danny had barely spoken to her all week. Stephanie knew he was still angry that she had surprised him with the reunion. She hoped he would get over it soon.

Stephanie headed into the kitchen.

To her surprise, Danny sat at the table, reading. She almost wished she could sneak back upstairs without his seeing her.

"Stephanie, can I talk to you?" Danny said. To her surprise, her father's voice was gentle. There was no hint of anger at all.

"Uh, sure, Dad," she said. She grabbed a handful of cookies, then joined her father at the kitchen table. When she sat down she realized what it was he had been reading. It was the story from the *Teen Weekender*, which had come out that morning. She must have left it on the table.

"I can't believe this," Danny said, staring at the magazine in front of him.

Stephanie swallowed nervously. How could she have been so dumb as to leave the story out where her father could find it? Surely he must be angry, reading about how she and Tamar thought his feud with Ben was "ridiculous."

"Dad, I can explain—"

"Steph, this story is . . . *terrific*," Danny said.

"Terrific?" Stephanie repeated. "I . . . I thought you would be mad."

Danny shook his head. "No. I'm not mad. At least, not mad at you," he said. "What I'm mad about is how stupid I've been. Just like you said in your story—it's ridiculous."

"I'm sorry, I didn't mean—"

"No, what you wrote was true," Danny protested. "Don't apologize. What you did—trying to bring me and Ben together like that—was a wonderful thing."

"But you were so angry at me last Saturday," Stephanie reminded him.

Danny laughed. "I was furious! And I was still angry at you the rest of the week . . . even up until a little while ago. Then I read this story and it hit me like a ton of bricks: this whole feud between Ben and me—it's *stupid!*"

Stephanie couldn't believe her ears.

"As I was reading," her father went on, "I

couldn't believe how idiotic the whole thing seemed. Then I thought about you and Tamar. How you both worked so hard to make that day special and how I went and ruined it."

"You were just caught off guard, I guess," Stephanie offered.

"Maybe," Danny said, "but I still owe you an apology. I'm sorry I ruined your reunion, sweetheart."

He got up from the table and gave Stephanie a big hug.

"Thanks, Dad," Stephanie told him. "I'm just glad you're not mad at me anymore."

Danny sat back down. "You and Tamar obviously make a good team. But because of this fight between me and Ben, you never had a chance to get to know your own cousin."

"Well, you and Ben must still have a lot in common," Stephanie said. "Because even though Tamar and I never knew each other, we're practically twins. We like all the same things, and we're both great writers."

Danny smiled. "Maybe you're right," he said. "Maybe Ben and I have raised our kids the same way. We always did agree on everything . . . until the big fight."

"Well, Tamar and I have promised each other

that we're never going to fight again," Stephanie said.

Danny looked at her thoughtfully. "You know what?" he asked. "That's a good idea."

Stephanie watched as her father walked over to the phone and picked up the receiver. He pushed a few buttons, then waited.

"Ben?" he said, his voice shaking slightly. "It's me, Danny."

CHAPTER
15

◆ ◀ ✦ ◆

Stephanie was proud of the decorations she had chosen for the second Tanner family reunion—she and Tamar had managed to find the perfect shade of green balloons to match the Tanner family reunion number two T-shirts.

She gazed around the Hillside Park picnic area, and a huge smile crept across her face.

"This is the best picnic *ever*," Tamar said, grabbing her second turkey sandwich and sitting on the bench next to Stephanie. "And the park looks even better than it did for the first Tanner family reunion!" she added with a laugh.

"That's for sure!" Stephanie agreed. "Everyone's having such a good time. Isn't it great?"

Stephanie watched happily as her family and Tamar's family got along so well. At the next table D.J. was engaged in a heavy conversation with Tamar's older brother, Brian, telling him all about life at college.

Over on a blanket on the grass, Michelle led the younger kids, Nicky, Alex, and Tamar's little brother, Stephen, in a game of Duck, Duck, Goose.

Joey, Jesse, Becky, and Tamar's mother, Liz, were sharing spinach pie at the next picnic table.

Sitting on a park bench away from the others were her father and Ben.

Stephanie watched how her dad smiled and laughed as he spoke to his cousin. She was sure they were busy catching up on the past twenty years.

"I'm so glad your father called last week," Tamar said, handing Stephanie a can of iced tea. "When my dad told me Danny had just called him and they had made up, I couldn't believe it! After twenty years, all it took was someone saying, 'I'm sorry'!"

"Can you imagine?" Stephanie said. "The

whole Big Cousins Incident was over a *misunder-standing!*"

"I know," Tamar replied. "I can't believe your father thought my father *stole* his speech. All he really did was hand in the wrong copy of the speech by accident. He didn't even realize he had done it until graduation day."

Stephanie giggled. "He must have been shocked when he stood up to read his speech and realized it was the one my dad had written and not his!"

"If only they had talked it out then," Tamar said thoughtfully, "they would have realized it was a simple mistake. They could have been friends for all these years. And we could have met when we were babies!"

"At least they're talking now," Stephanie said.

"Yeah, and it was our article that got them back together," Tamar said.

Stephanie pulled her copy of *Teen Weekender* from her Sport- Glo pack and laid it on the picnic table in front of her.

"It *was* a great story!" Tamar remarked as she munched on her sandwich and read over Stephanie's shoulder.

Stephanie nodded. "Yup, the story was pretty great!" she agreed. "We were just lucky Miss Stetson was willing to give us another chance."

"Absolutely!" Tamar agreed.

"Still . . . the story wasn't the *best* part!" Stephanie added.

Tamar stopped chewing and stared at her cousin. Then a smile broke out across her face.

"Nope, it wasn't the best part!" she said.

The two girls hunched over the copy of *Teen Weekender* and admired the fabulous picture of them hugging on the cover.

"Now *that's* what I call a great cover story!" Stephanie exclaimed. "In fact, it was so great that I had to buy these." She opened her Sport-Glo pack to reveal fifty more copies!

Tamar cracked up. She reached over and opened her own Sport-Glo pack. Just like Stephanie's, it was stuffed with copies of *Teen Weekender.*

Stephanie couldn't help but laugh.

Twice the Tanner, she thought, *twice the fun!*

Full House™

SISTERS

A brand-new series starring Stephanie AND Michelle!

#1 Two On The Town

Stephanie and Michelle find themselves
in the big city—and in big trouble!

#2 One Boss Too Many

Stephanie and Michelle think camp will be major fun.
If only these two sisters were getting along!

When sisters get together...expect the unexpected!

A MINSTREL® BOOK
Published by Pocket Books

2012-01

FULL HOUSE™
Club Stephanie

Summer is here and Stephanie is ready for some fun!

#1 Fun, Sun, and Flamingoes

#2 Fireworks and Flamingoes

#3 Flamingo Revenge

-All Now Available-

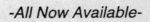

A MINSTREL BOOK
Published by Pocket Books

1357-03

FULL HOUSE™
Michelle

A MINSTREL® BOOK
Published by Pocket Books

1033-30

FULL HOUSE Stephanie™

PHONE CALL FROM A FLAMINGO	88004-7/$3.99
THE BOY-OH-BOY NEXT DOOR	88121-3/$3.99
TWIN TROUBLES	88290-2/$3.99
HIP HOP TILL YOU DROP	88291-0/$3.99
HERE COMES THE BRAND NEW ME	89858-2/$3.99
THE SECRET'S OUT	89859-0/$3.99
DADDY'S NOT-SO-LITTLE GIRL	89860-4/$3.99
P.S. FRIENDS FOREVER	89861-2/$3.99
GETTING EVEN WITH THE FLAMINGOES	52273-6/$3.99
THE DUDE OF MY DREAMS	52274-4/$3.99
BACK-TO-SCHOOL COOL	52275-2/$3.99
PICTURE ME FAMOUS	52276-0/$3.99
TWO-FOR-ONE CHRISTMAS FUN	53546-3/$3.99
THE BIG FIX-UP MIX-UP	53547-1/$3.99
TEN WAYS TO WRECK A DATE	53548-X/$3.99
WISH UPON A VCR	53549-8/$3.99
DOUBLES OR NOTHING	56841-8/$3.99
SUGAR AND SPICE ADVICE	56842-6/$3.99
NEVER TRUST A FLAMINGO	56843-4/$3.99
THE TRUTH ABOUT BOYS	00361-5/$3.99
CRAZY ABOUT THE FUTURE	00362-3/$3.99
MY SECRET ADMIRER	00363-1/$3.99
BLUE RIBBON CHRISTMAS	00830-7/$3.99
THE STORY ON OLDER BOYS	00831-5/$3.99
MY THREE WEEKS AS A SPY	00832-3/$3.99
NO BUSINESS LIKE SHOW BUSINESS	01725-X/$3.99
MAIL-ORDER BROTHER	01726-8/$3.99
TO CHEAT OR NOT TO CHEAT	01727-6/$3.99
WINNING IS EVERYTHING	02098-6/$3.99
HELLO BIRTHDAY, GOOD-BYE FRIEND	02160-5/$3.99
THE ART OF KEEPING SECRETS	02161-3/$3.99

Available from Minstrel® Books Published by Pocket Books